# THE ROOMMATE

KIERSTEN MODGLIN

KIERSTEN
MODGLIN
love loss thrills

www.kierstenmodglinauthor.com
Cover Design: Tadpole Designs
Editing: Three Owls Editing
Proofreading: My Brother's Editor
Formatting: Tadpole Designs
First Print Edition: 2021
First Electronic Edition: 2021

*This one's to the adults who never outgrew reading past bedtime...*

# CHAPTER ONE

Nothing says regret quite like shaving your neck with a dollar-store razor in front of a filmy mirror in a rent-by-the-week motel.

When Addy asked me to move out, I thought I'd be in the motel for just a few nights. She needed that time to cool down after our latest fight, I knew, but could it really be that bad? We were *us,* after all. We always came through. No matter how bad our fights had been in the past, we'd always found a way to stick together.

But this time was different. I just hadn't known it until more nights had passed without her inviting me to come home.

I'd spent most of the last three weeks in denial about what was happening, but as I grazed the razor blade across my stubble-covered chin, it hit me.

*I might never go back home.*

I might never spend another night in the house we'd picked out, surrounded by the things we'd accumulated in our nineteen years together. I might never again live under the same roof with my wife and daughter.

We hadn't said the words yet, hadn't decided how we were going to divide up the marital assets or how custody of Rory would work, but the reality sat unspoken between us. If I didn't find a way to fix things soon, she'd let me go forever. I'd crossed the line one too many times, missed one too many dinners, forgotten one too many birthdays.

I loved my job, had worked hard for my job, but it had ruined my life.

I wanted to fix things, but I had no idea how. I'd tried calling her, but the calls went unanswered. When I stopped by, she wouldn't come to the door, or, when she did, she'd say I needed to leave.

The house was in both our names, I knew. I had the keys; it wasn't as if she'd changed the locks, but I was no longer welcome there. She'd made it clear that only one of us could stay. Her or me. And it had to be her. I didn't want her to leave the home we'd shared, and I didn't want to ask her to move into her mother's new, tiny two-bedroom condo, though Addy had offered multiple times. I knew my mother-in-law would be all too happy to have Addy and Rory stay there for a while, but it felt wrong to me. This wasn't Addy's fault. My wife had done every-thing she could to fix us, and now it was up to me. The truth was, though, neither of us could really afford to stay in the house alone for long.

I knew we'd end up having to sell it, if it came down to it, but I didn't want that. We'd built a life there. It was the home we'd celebrated every bit of our success in over the last five years—promotions, birthday parties, anniversaries, new deals being closed. It was the home where Rory's beloved Dalmatian had been buried in the backyard, and where the rotting tree house we'd spent our first night at the house in sat, still waiting for me to repair it. It was the home where I'd had chance after chance to appreciate how quickly time was passing, how fast my daughter was growing up, how rapidly my wife and I were growing apart, but had chosen not to. Not because I didn't care, but because I never took it seriously enough. I never thought I was really risking losing them.

I knew I needed to do better, and I would. I swore that I would if only she'd give me a chance.

But I'd made that promise before, and it meant little to her at that point. She didn't trust me. I'd spent the last five years giving her reason after reason not to rely on me.

I used a towel to wipe the rest of the shaving cream from my neck, looking over the razor-burned skin carefully. I needed to shop for new supplies, including a shaving cream that wasn't provided by the motel staff. But doing so meant that I had decided I was going to be there for a while, and I was far from admitting that, even to myself. If I held out, I was holding on to hope. How much longer could I do that?

I couldn't keep showing up to work with red, irritated skin and unstyled hair. I'd made due with what little I'd managed to grab on my way out of the house that night and what the front desk could provide for free during my stay, but I was at a *motel*, not a *hotel*, and resources were limited. I could no longer put off a trip to the grocery store.

As it was Saturday and my first meeting of the day

didn't start until early afternoon, I decided I'd run across town and try to grab a few things. I might even call Addy and see if I could pick anything up for the house, maybe get an afternoon with Rory. It had been three weeks; the least she could do was allow me an afternoon with our daughter.

After applying some of the unscented moisturizing cream on my neck, I tossed the towel onto the floor and walked out of the room, flicking off the light as I went. I dressed in front of the small, double-paned window that overlooked the vast expanse of the parking lot, littered with browning leaves and rusted vehicles. Everything here was old, falling apart. The motel was where things came to die.

Marriages included.

Once I'd gotten dressed, I pulled on my black jacket and tennis shoes and headed out the door, double-checking that the room key was safely in the pocket of my jeans. I jogged down the rickety stairs, each step creating a loud thud and the creak of metal that I'd grown to expect.

God, I needed to get out of that place and back to my home.

Thirty minutes later, I was walking down the aisle of a midtown grocery store, a basket hanging from my arm as I tossed a box of protein bars and Atkins shakes on top of the shampoo, body wash, replacement razor, shaving cream, and air fresheners. I would only buy what would fit in the basket. Anything else would last too long, and I couldn't afford to stay much longer. Emotionally or financially.

I rounded the corner of the aisle, nearly running into someone, and stepped back quickly.

"My bad, sorry."

"Oops, sorry about that," he said at the same time. We both laughed as he turned sideways to allow me to pass. I smiled at him, ducking my head gently, and he met my eye so I could get a better look at him. He was tall and thin, an apostrophe-shaped scar just above his right, over-grown eyebrow, and his smile spread wide, revealing small, rounded teeth. I met his light blue eyes from behind the thick glasses that rested on his sharp, pointed nose, noticing that he looked vaguely familiar, though I couldn't place him.

Just as the thought swam through my brain, his smile grew wider, his small eyes lighting up. *"Wesley Gates?"*

I sucked in a sharp breath as he said my name. So, I wasn't imagining it. I really did know him from…somewhere. But where? I tried to place him quickly, racking my brain for some semblance of a clue. How did I know that face? Was he the friend of a client? Had I met him at a party or marketing event? Where did I know him from? He looked young. Younger than me, perhaps, but when he smiled, I saw the vague hint of wrinkles near his eyes that led me to believe he may have been older than he initially appeared.

I felt the heat rush to my cheeks, revealing my embar-rassment before I could staunch it. I met so many people at the many parties I attended for work—artists, managers, songwriters, crew, drivers, security, and even fans. I'd become better at memorizing faces over the years. Time had proven that even the most seemingly inconsequential person could refer a client to me, or become a client themselves.

"Hey, *man*," I said, albeit lamely, "it's good to see you. Sorry, you're catching me a little bit distracted."

He gave a dry laugh, patting my shoulder with a surprisingly powerful grip. "Oh, wow. It's so good to see you, too. How long has it been? Fifteen, twenty years, give or take? How've you been? Do you still live around here?"

I tried to calculate. Fifteen years meant he wasn't anyone from work, as fifteen years ago I was still in college, not yet an agent. Twenty years ago, I was still in high school. Which was it? "I do, yeah. In Green Hills. What about you?"

"Green Hills?" he asked, his jaw dropping slightly and his voice breathless, obviously impressed. It was the reaction I was used to getting whenever I gave anyone my address, despite the fact that we were drowning in debt to be able to live there, and if I couldn't stop my impending divorce, the address wouldn't be ours for much longer. Still, I smiled as if there were no worries plaguing me. I'd become wildly successful at pretending to have it all. "Rubbin' elbows with the rich and fancy, eh? No wonder I haven't seen you around." He let out a dry laugh again, almost a cough. "Yeah, I've got an apartment a few blocks from here. What are you doing on this side of town anyway?" His eyes drifted to the basket in my hands.

I instinctively tucked it closer to my side. "Oh, just working. I have a few client meetings downtown this afternoon, and I needed a few things."

"Oh, yeah? Where are you working?"

"I'm a booking agent for the Noel DeMarcum Agency." The amount of pride I had when saying those words had never waned. I'd worked my way up from an assistant to an agent in just under ten years, and it was the one thing in my life I hadn't managed to screw up.

"No shit? Wow." The wrinkle in his forehead grew closer to the dusty blond hair atop his head. "Here I was feeling good about telling you I run my own business, but you've one-upped me again, Gates. Congrats." His smile was stiff but friendly.

"You own your own business, though? That's amazing. You're your own boss, hm? Very cool."

"Are you going to ask what I do?" The smile shifted from stiff to amused and, right then and there, I almost clasped onto who he was. Er, okay, not *who* he was, but where I knew him from. It was as if the answer had floated to the surface of my brain and then been dragged back down before it could fully form. We'd gone to high school together, I wanted to say. I recognized him—probably from a party or a class...or maybe I was thinking of college, after all? His features were so familiar, it was driving me crazy. I could picture him, then, but the edges of the memory were fuzzy. Why couldn't I place his face with a name? I'd never been good with names, but usually I could at least figure out where I knew the person from. Why was he so elusive?

He cleared his throat, interrupting my thoughts, and I shook my head. "S-sorry. Yeah, of course. What do you do?"

"I work in IT, freelancing for companies all over the city." He said it as if the wind had been taken from his sails, and I instantly felt guilty. "I dabble a bit in software development, but it's mostly just cybersecurity."

"Very cool, man. I'm lost on all that technology stuff. I still have to Google how to find certain things on my iPhone."

That seemed to make him feel a bit better, and he grinned. "Well, if you ever need any help, I'm around."

"Thanks," I said, tapping the pocket where my phone rested. "I may just take you up on that."

He inhaled sharply, shifting a half step back. "Well, you said you have meetings to get to, right? I should probably let you go."

I glanced at the Apple Watch on my wrist and nodded. "Yeah, I've got to get this stuff to the office and check on Addison, but it was—"

"Addison?" he asked, his teeth peeking out from between the thin lips again. His eyes gleamed at me. "You're still with Addison Taylor?"

The sound of her name sent pain tearing through my stomach, but I stayed still and emotionless. "Addison Gates now—" *Probably not for much longer...* "But, yeah, we'll have been married sixteen years next month." How was it possible he remembered the name of my then girl-friend, but I couldn't even recall his name?

"Wow. Congratulations to you. I knew you two were serious back then, but I had no idea you'd actually end up together long term. What's she up to these days?"

Something about the way he said it, or maybe the look in his eye, made my stomach flip. How did he know

Addy, besides from school? Had they been close? If she were here, I had no doubt she would know who he was. That was just who Addy was. Her kindness soaked through in the form of making sure everyone felt included, important. It was why she made such an amazing teacher. "She teaches at Willow Grove Academy."

He glanced up, seemingly lost in thought, before saying, slowly, as if he were expelling air through the plug of an air mattress, "Wow, good for her."

It was my turn to nod stiffly. "Yep."

"Well, anyway, I'll let you go. Give Addison my best, will you? And, seriously, if you ever need help with your phone or...technology in general, or if you just want to grab a beer sometime, I'm always around. It'd be great to catch up."

"Yeah, I'd like that," I said, sidestepping to make my way around him. "It was great to see you."

"You too," he said with a casual wave. "See you around."

*Not likely.* I checked out without adding anything else to my basket, my mind too consumed with figuring out who he was. As I walked to my car, I pulled out the keys to my silver BMW and got inside, speeding out of the parking lot and toward the outskirts of downtown to get onto the interstate.

The entire way home, I thought only of the man, trying desperately to place him. Had he been Addy's friend? Was that why I knew him? Or had he just been another face in a crowded classroom? It felt like more than that. His features were so burned into my memory. It was on the tip of my tongue, and yet, I couldn't quite figure it out.

As I pulled into the paved driveway of our two-story, white-brick home, he was still on my mind. The house was modest compared to most of the ones in our subdivision, with outdated features and less than a quarter of an acre, without a pool or fenced-in yard, but we'd still gone nearly a million dollars into debt to call it ours.

We liked our neighborhood, liked that our neighbors were all much older than us and mostly kept to themselves, and we liked Rory's school. But as the property taxes rose exponentially each year, the financial struggles had become more prominent. It was one of the leading causes of our fights. The house was my idea. I wanted to fit in at work. I wanted to host parties and extend dinner invitations without feeling self-conscious about where we lived. If it were up to Addison, we'd have bought something less gaudy in an older neighborhood farther from downtown. Something with half the price tag and double the space. But, as usual, I'd won the argument.

My ability to win, to cause my opponent to concede, had always been something I'd taken great pride in, but I knew now how it had made Addison feel. Always giving up and giving in, she'd lost a part of herself. I'd argued it right out of her. I needed to fix that.

I approached the door, staring into the two-story, black-paned window that looked directly into the foyer as I knocked and, within moments, my wife's shadow passed over the white tile of the floor before she came into view. It was another perk of our neighborhood: we were one of the few places on earth where people still answered the door without scurrying across the floor to peek through the blinds first. In fact, most of the homes in the neighborhood had similar large windows and glass-paned doors, giving everyone a clear view into each other's homes and lives. When we'd first moved in, it had taken some getting used to, but now it seemed perfectly normal until I drove through different neighborhoods and realized not everyone lived that way.

When Addison saw me through the glass, the fake smile on her face fell away. She opened the door, dressed in bright green spandex pants that she'd pulled over her soft stomach and a thin, gray tank top. Her blonde, natural curls had been pulled away from her face into a ponytail, her face clean and free of makeup.

"What are you doing here, Wes?" My name was a curse word on her lips. Whenever she called me by name, rather than *babe* or *honey*, I had either disappointed or royally pissed her off.

I didn't try to step inside, and she didn't move out of the way to let me through. Instead, I adjusted in place on my own porch—on a welcome mat *I'd* picked out.

"Is Rory home? I was hoping I could see her today."

"Why didn't you call?" she asked with a sigh and the wrinkle of her button nose. "I could've saved you a trip. She's not here."

"I didn't call because you wouldn't have answered." I huffed, but I changed my tone back to a hint of pleasantry quickly. "Why isn't she here?"

"It's Saturday. She's out with friends."

"Which friends?"

She pinched the bridge of her nose as if the question

was ridiculous. "Tessa's parents took them to their beach house in Naples for the weekend."

"I thought we agreed we didn't want her hanging around with Tessa."

"That was Terra. Tessa is the one we like—Doug and Caity's daughter. Remember? The ones that own the car washes all around town?"

"Right," I said as I recalled who she was talking about. "Sorry. Yeah. That makes sense."

"So…" She stepped back just a hair, her hand resting on the wood of the door. "Is there anything else I can do for you? I should get back to…" She didn't finish her sentence, but simply stared at me as if she'd said enough.

"Actually, yeah. I was hoping I could come in for a second. There are a few things I want to talk to you about." My chest tightened with anticipation. I couldn't read her. Was she going to tell me to get lost? Would she open the door and let me inside? Thus far, she'd spent her time telling me that she needed space. We hadn't carried on a conversation for more than five minutes in the three weeks since I'd left. *Er, been kicked out.*

She glanced over her shoulder, and a cold thought filled my mind. Did she have company? Was there another man inside my home? I fought the urge to clench my fists.

"Sure," she said finally, stepping back a half step and allowing me to cross over the threshold. The house smelled the same as it always had; my absence hadn't changed it. There was the vague hint of the Spring Breeze laundry detergent and fabric softener Addy ordered weekly, the lemon Pledge we used to polish the wood furniture, the peach shampoo she washed her hair with.

It was uniquely us, and yet, even without me, it carried on.

They carried on.

"I don't have a lot of time. I have a few errands to run later this afternoon," Addy said as she led the way into the kitchen.

I followed closely behind her. "This won't take much —" As I rounded the corner, my words ended abruptly as I stared at the person on the other side of our oversized island, square in the middle of our kitchen. "Hello, Vivienne. I didn't realize you were here."

My mother-in-law, a tall, lean woman with short, gray hair and bright blue eyes, stared across the room at me, her jaw tight. We'd never had the best relationship, but Vivienne had never been cruel. I wondered what she thought of me now. What my wife had told her about where it had all gone wrong.

"Hello, Wesley. I didn't realize you were either." The wrinkles around her eyes deepened as she narrowed her gaze at me, lifting the mug of coffee in front of her to her lips with both hands. "Addy didn't mention she was expecting you."

"I wasn't expecting him," she said, then glanced at me over her shoulder, pulling open the stainless steel door of the refrigerator and grabbing a carton of almond milk. "Mom and I are going shopping together this afternoon." She popped the lid off of the clear smoothie cup she'd had waiting on the island and added in the milk, turning back toward the refrigerator to grab the mango, pre-chopped pineapple, and a bag of spinach. "So, what can I do for you? Is something wrong?"

"I, um," my eyes darted between Vivienne and Addy, heat flushing my cheeks, "I wanted to see if you thought I could see Rory this weekend."

"I've already told you she's with Tessa." She tossed in the pineapple and mango, tapping her fingernails against the laminate countertop. Vivienne watched the encounter closely, making no move to shield her gaze.

I looked her way, feeling the heat climbing the nape of my neck. "Right, I, um—"

"Mom, do you mind giving us just a minute?" Addy asked, stopping the quiet humming I hadn't noticed coming from Vivienne's lips.

She nodded gently and took a step back with her mug of coffee. "Yes, sorry. Don't mind me. I'll finish this on the patio." She moved to the counter and dug through the black purse that rested atop it, producing a plum-colored Kindle and wagging it in the air. "If I don't see you before you leave, it was good to see you, Wesley."

"You too," I said halfheartedly. She left the room, and I listened as her footsteps descended down the hall, and then heard the back door open and shut. When we were left with only silence, I cleared my throat again, picking up the conversation where we'd left off. "I realize she's with Tessa today, but I'm wondering if we could get some kind of schedule worked out. I mean, could I see her next weekend? If you aren't going to let me come home, I want to figure out when I'll be able to see my daughter next."

"Well, that depends. Have you gotten your own place?" she asked, resting a hand on the countertop with an exhausted look in her eyes.

My heart sank. *My own place?* "No, not yet. I...I mean, I

was waiting to see what you wanted me to do. It's not that serious yet, is it? I mean, for me to get my own place, I'd need to sign a lease. That would mean at least a year apart —I might get lucky with six months, but there's no guarantee. Do you really think we're ready to commit to that? A lot can happen in a year."

"I hear what you're saying, but if you want to see her, it really seems like our only option. That's why I'd offered for Rory and me to move in with Mom. You could move back here, and—"

"I've told you I don't want that. This is Rory's home. It's your home. I don't want to uproot you both. It's not an option."

She pursed her lips. "I understand that. And I appreciate it, but Rory doesn't want to come visit you at that motel, and I don't blame her. I could probably talk her into spending the day with you if you want to take her shopping or something, but she's not going to come stay with you, Wes. Not at that place."

"It's not like I want to be there either. It's not exactly my dream." I steadied my breathing, watching as she ran her hands over a few stray pieces of her blonde hair. She tried to tuck them back into her ponytail carefully, busying herself with the smoothie once again. "You didn't answer my question," I pointed out. "Do you think we're ready to commit to a year apart? Why can't I just move back in and stay in the guest room? The only reason I can think of is if you're sure we're not going to be able to work things out. Is that what this is? Is this…are we done?"

"Wes, look…" She hung her head down, inhaling

deeply, her shoulders hunched. "I know you aren't ready for this conversation, but nothing has changed for me"— my heart leapt—"since the night I asked you to leave"— and fell again. "I don't know if there's a future for us, but I don't see it right now. I don't see it in the next few months, or even in the next year. I'm sorry. I know that's not what you wanted to hear, but I want you to get your own place. If you don't want us to move in with Mom, you need to get yourself settled in somewhere. Someplace with enough space for Rory to visit. Someplace with enough room for your things. We have to start moving forward in one direction or the other."

Just like that, I was back there the night of our last fight. I relived the moment she'd asked me to move out with tears streaming down her cheeks. The missed dinner reservations. The silent house I'd walked into, flipping on the light to find her sitting in the dark, staring across the room. She was empty. Emotionless. I'd done that to her.

"I know I hurt you, Addy. I know I messed up, but come on. We aren't *there*. It isn't that bad. We can still fix this."

"The fact that you can even say that to me with a straight face proves that we aren't in the same marriage, Wes. We *are* that bad. *This bad.* We've fallen apart. I can't tell you how many nights I've waited up for you, how many soccer games and spelling bees and parents nights you've missed for our daughter. You pulled her away from her friends so we could live here. You pulled me away from a career I loved—"

"How can you say that? You're still a teacher—"

"I loved what I was doing there, though, Wes. I loved

teaching at my old school. This place, this area—it's not me. It's not *us.* But you don't see that. You never have. You wanted to be here because you wanted to fit in with the people you work with, and you know what? Congratulations, *you* do! But *we* don't. You promised me when we moved here nothing would change, but everything has changed. Including you. Rory is starving herself and being bullied at school for liking sports more than shopping, and you couldn't make time in your schedule to come to even a single therapy session for her—"

"I said I was sorry for that. You know I tried to make it—"

"Yes, I know you were sorry. I know you *are* sorry. You're always sorry, Wes. But at some point, sorry stops being enough."

"Let me go now. Let me take her. I'll do whatever you want—"

"I don't need you to go now, Wes," she said, cutting me off. "We both needed you *then.* The point is that so much has gone wrong since we've moved here, and we aren't happy anymore. Between Rory's health and her being bullied, and the fact that you've made me start going to these lavish yoga studios and gala events, even though I'd much rather be running bake sales with the kids back home and helping tutor after school. You want us to be these new versions of ourselves, versions you envisioned, but I liked who we used to be. Rory and I loved what we had before, and you took that away from us."

I stepped toward her. "You can't put all of that on me. You agreed—"

She put a hand on my chest, stopping me from going

any further. "I did. I did agree. I've always wanted what was best for you. I wanted you to be happy, and I thought that would make me happy enough. I'm not trying to play the martyr here, Wes. You're correct that I agreed to this move and all that it entailed. I knew what this zip code, this house, this career meant to you." She pressed her lips together, huffing out a breath. "I just never realized they meant more to you than we do."

I recoiled, my heart thudding in my ears. "*They don't.* You know that's ridiculous. You two mean everything to me. How can you even say that?"

"If that were the case, you would've skipped a meeting or dinner, or managed to make it home on time once over the past seven months when I needed to talk to you about what was going on. With us...with Rory. Instead, I've had to deal with it all on my own. I just can't live like this anymore, Wes. If you want me to stay here, Rory to stay here, then you need to get your own place so we can start the next steps of this process. I'm not trying to take Rory away from you. She loves you, and I know how much you care about her. I want her to be able to visit you—that's not what this is about. I just want some semblance of normalcy, and visiting her father at some shoddy, run-down motel downtown isn't normal."

"But us being apart is? Or you moving her into your mom's cramped condo? Look, I get it, okay? I hear you. I hear what you're saying. I messed up, and I want to fix it, but...Addy," I lifted my hand and brushed a piece of hair from her face. She remained still, not stopping me. "I love you. I love you and Rory more than anything in this world. If you want to move back to LaVergne, we can. If you want to sell this house and buy something smaller, if you want to go back to your old school—whatever you want, we'll do it. I just need you to talk to me."

"I've tried—"

"I know you've tried. I get it. I'm sorry I haven't been here more. I'm sorry, okay? I've—" I cocked my head to the side, studying her and hoping to see a softness in her eyes or less tension in her neck, but she remained steady. "Addy, I've loved you longer than I ever lived without loving you. You're a part of me, and I'm a part of you. We can't just let that go because we hit a rough patch, can we? I've loved you from the time I was sixteen years old. I don't know how to exist without you."

"But that's just it, Wes. You have been. We've shared a bed, passed each other in the hallway, traded off laundry duty, but that's been it for more than a year now. We aren't *existing* together anymore. You've been gone for a long time, and I'm really hurt by it. It doesn't mean I don't love you, I just need time to figure out where my head is."

"So, your solution to us being too distant is to have me move out?" I asked with a scoff.

She shook her head, barely looking at me as she popped a piece of pineapple in her mouth before dumping the spinach in a bowl and heading for the sink. "You don't get it."

"No, I really don't. There's one thing we can agree on. I never realized we were having problems at all, let alone ones bad enough to cause us to separate or, God forbid, get a *divorce.*" I whispered the word as if it were a profanity. "Rory needs both of us. I don't want to do this to her. We have to find a way to work this out." I moved toward her, placing my hand on the small of her back. She'd told me once it made her feel safe to have my hand there. As my skin rested on the fabric of her tank top, she looked up at me, and I caught a glimpse of sadness there for the first time. "Just let me come home. Please. Please don't do this. I'll do whatever you want… I'll take Rory to therapy. I'll stay in the guest bedroom indefinitely. I'll be home before dinner every night. Hell, I'll *make* dinner every night. We can talk as much as you want. I can take a week off, and we can reconnect. What will it take?" My eyes danced between hers, begging her to tell me something tangible I could do to make this all okay.

"You don't get it." She shook her head, breaking eye contact and turning back to the spinach as she ran it under the faucet, bouncing it under the water in our metal strainer. "I hear what you're saying, and I know you're trying. It's not that I don't appreciate it, because I do. It's just that…I know you think it's what I want to hear, and maybe it is, but you can't just…do that. I'm not a client or a deal, where you can just negotiate terms until I give in. For months, Wes, *for months* I asked you to meet me for dinner or to spend a weekend at home so we could reconnect. I asked you to spend more time with Rory. I asked you to take a week off so we could all get away. I told you how badly we were struggling, how much we needed to discuss everything, and you chose to ignore it. Or worse, you'd hear me and still refuse to act. Or you'd promise things would get better and then make no effort to see it through—"

"I hear you now," I told her, reaching for her hair

again, but this time, she jerked backward, shut off the faucet, and carried the spinach back to the island.

"You aren't hearing me, though, Wes. That's the point. I'm telling you that I need space. I need time to figure everything out, and you're refusing to listen, even now. Even knowing that *you not listening to me* is what brought us here."

I rested my hand on the edge of the sink, the cold stainless steel against my palm. There was a time when I would've argued with her, but the truth was, I did hear her. I understood what she was saying. I knew I'd messed up and offered more apologies and excuses than actual solutions or effort. I knew she wanted time to clear her head, but that wasn't what I wanted. I wanted to be home. I wanted to see her and Rory every day, even if they weren't ready to forgive me. I wanted to prove how sorry I was, how much I hated what I'd done. I wanted to fight for what we'd built rather than back away and wait for further instruction. It just wasn't in me. I was a fighter. Determination ran in my blood; it was all that I knew.

She had her back to me, and I watched her shoulders rise and fall with heavy breaths as she finished combining the ingredients for her smoothie into the cup.

"Well, there's nothing I can say to change your mind then, obviously. I guess I'll pack a few more of my things," I said slowly, hoping she'd say that wasn't necessary. Instead, she nodded, then spun around, and walked straight toward me. For a moment, I stood still, lost in her eyes as she approached me. When she cleared her throat, smoothie cup in hand, I realized what she wanted and stepped out of the way so she could start up the single-serve blender that prepared her breakfast every morning.

"I think that would be good," she said, no longer meeting my eye as she pressed the button to start the machine.

I nodded, not totally comprehending what she was saying. "O-okay." I moved away from her, my entire body numb. How was it possible? How had it happened?

When I reached the door, I spun back around. "Hey, I ran into someone at the store today…"

She shut off the blender and looked over her shoulder at me. "Huh?"

"I ran into someone from school. He knew you."

She waited for me to say something else, but I wasn't sure what I wanted to say.

"Okay?"

"I don't know who he was. He was tall and thin with light brownish-blond hair. He seemed to have been close to you and said to tell you hi."

She shrugged, pulling the cup away from the blender and shaking it. "That doesn't exactly narrow it down. He didn't tell you his name?"

"No, he acted like he knew me, but by the time I realized I had no idea who he was, I was too embarrassed to ask. I thought he might've been someone I'd met through work, but he remembered you too, so it had to be school. I'm assuming college, but I don't know that for sure. He remembered me straight away—my name and everything."

"Well, that wouldn't be hard," she said, and I noticed a hint of warmth in her tone.

I eyed her, my thoughts totally free of the man in an instant. Was she flirting with me? "What does that mean?"

"You weren't easy to forget, Wes. You know that. Track star, top of our class, popular with everything and everyone… There isn't a person we went to school with who wouldn't know who you were."

I felt my lips turning up into a smile I couldn't fight. Her eyes trailed up my body, as if she was remembering who we once were, and then landed on my face. She sighed, her shoulders heaving with the breath, and pointed toward the door on the opposite side of the room.

"I should go check on Mom. Feel free to pack whatever you need. And if you want me to ask Rory to stay home next Saturday, maybe the two of you could get out and do something together. No promises, but I can try to clear her schedule."

Coldness swept through me, and I swallowed, taking a half step back as her words registered. The look in her eye a moment ago was gone, and we were back to business. I nodded. "Right… Okay. Yeah, sure, I'll let you know."

"We'll probably head to the store in a few minutes, but don't feel rushed. Just let yourself out if we're already gone. Don't forget to lock up behind you."

"Will do," I said, my voice powerless as she turned away from me and walked out of the room. I let my shoulders fall, my chest heavy with frustration and sorrow as I turned away from her and headed down the hall toward the bedroom we'd once shared.

I tried not to look at the pictures of us on the bedroom walls—pictures from happier days—as I packed a bag, fighting back tears as they blurred my vision. The photographs hadn't been taken down, which told me she hadn't given up completely, but her words told a different story. She wanted me to get my own place. She wanted me to build a life without her.

My marriage was over.

My life was over.

And I had no one to blame but myself.

If only I'd known my problems had just begun.

# CHAPTER TWO

Once Addy and Vivienne had left the house, I decided to treat myself to a shower under the rainfall showerhead I'd had installed two Christmases back. I lathered up, washing and rinsing under the falling water as I tried not to think of the time Addy and I had spent together right where I stood. Admittedly, those times had become less frequent over the past few years, since I'd accepted my most recent promotion, but was she right? Hadn't I made an effort to make her a priority? I had to work to provide for us, same as she did, but it didn't change the way I felt about her.

I loved Addy. I'd never stopped loving her. Didn't she know that? My wife had never been needy. We'd been together so long that we didn't require constant reassurance that things were okay and we were still good. So, when had that changed? And why hadn't I realized it?

I couldn't recall missing that many dinners or dates, though I knew there had been a few. She'd asked me to attend things that conflicted with work, or told me to take the weekend off when I was right in the middle of a contract negotiation, or asked if we could go out of town on vacation when things were too busy. Missing Rory's appointments was one of the worst things I'd done, but both times I'd believed my excuses were valid. Refusing to attend the conflicting staff meeting or to fly to Seattle in order to assist with a deal that had almost fallen through might've cost me my job. Even still, I should've tried harder for my marriage. For my daughter. I'd failed them both, even with the best of intentions. That was evident now. But she'd never told me she was on the verge of leaving. She'd never made it clear that her requests weren't merely requests, but demands with consequences.

Had I known, I would've done more. I would've fought harder. Now, here I was trying to fight, and she was no longer interested. What was I supposed to do?

I stayed under the water, letting it run over me as I thought about all that had gone wrong and all that I needed to do to fix it, though I kept coming to a brick wall.

One thing was certain, Addy wanted me to get a place, and I couldn't stay at the motel much longer. I wanted to see my daughter, and if it would take getting an apartment, that's what I would do. I made the decision that as soon as I got back to the motel, I'd start searching real estate listings.

I turned off the water finally, begrudgingly, and stepped out of the shower, wrapping the towel around my waist and wiping a dry spot on the mirror.

I remembered the days when Addy used to leave me

messages drawn on our mirror after her shower, so that when I took mine, the steam would bring them back to life. *I love you. Have a good day. See you tonight. Happy Birthday. Happy Anniversary.* No matter what had been going on in our lives, her messages were a constant for so long. I wondered when they'd stopped. Why hadn't I noticed that then?

Without thinking, I traced my fingers across the foggy glass. *I still love you.*

I bit back at the anger toward myself as my vision blurred with tears, and I tapped my phone. I had just an hour until my meeting and still needed to get more of my things packed.

I walked from the bathroom and sank down onto the stool in front of her vanity, where she got ready every morning. I ran my fingers over her lipsticks and moisturizers. How many times had I walked past her getting ready without taking the time to appreciate her? Without telling her she was beautiful? It made me sick to think about all I'd once had that may now be taken away from me.

I grabbed the bag I'd pulled from the closet, already half full of clothes and hygiene items I'd taken from the bathroom, and snuck a picture of the two of us from the edge of her dresser. I tossed it inside, tucking it between two shirts so it wouldn't end up damaged.

Then, I put on clean, dry clothes and rubbed pomade through my hair, making sure to place my towel and dirty clothes into the hamper instead of leaving them on the floor like I so often did. I walked across the room, tucking the last of what would fit into the bag—a pair of running shoes, two hoodies, five ties, and two more dress shirts—inside, and zipped it up.

Before I left, I took a piece of paper from the notepad she kept next to the bed for random, late-night thoughts and jotted out a short note.

**Addy,**

**I'm sorry for whatever pain I've caused you. I'm sorry I didn't appreciate you enough or listen to you enough. I want you to know that I truly do hear you now. I understand that I hurt you, that I let you down, and I'm going to do better. I hear what you're asking from me, and I want to be the man you deserve. Even if you never forgive me, I'll work every day to prove to you how much I love you. Because I do, Addy. I love you so much. I'm going to get my own place. I'm going to work less and make time for Rory. Just please don't shut me out, okay? Don't give up on us.**

**Love,**

**Wes**

I laid the note on the bed and headed toward the door with the bag slung over my shoulder. As I walked through the house, I checked my phone, surprised to see a new Facebook friend request on the screen.

I opened the app and checked the name, recognizing the face of the man I'd run into at the grocery store. *Elias Munn.*

Suddenly, the memory came back to me with stunning clarity. I'd known Elias from high school, not college. I hadn't heard from him since graduation. We hadn't been friends then, by any stretch of the imagination. We ran in different circles, and while he focused on academics, I'd been more into sports. But times had changed, and who said we couldn't be friends now? When everyone else in my life seemed to want little to do with me, the idea of having a friend outside of work was incredibly appealing.

As I turned the key in the door, locking it up and sliding my phone into my pocket, I thought maybe Elias was exactly the kind of friend I needed. Someone who remembered who I'd once been, rather than someone who knew what I'd become.

When my meeting was over, I'd reach out to him.

# CHAPTER THREE

I walked into the bar fifteen minutes after I'd agreed to meet Elias for a beer. He'd been able to get together almost instantly. Not that I'd expected any different. Elias was never the most popular person. From what I could remember of him, he always seemed to be rather reclusive. I remembered him as the pimple-faced kid who'd tutored kids for extra cash on the weekends and skipped out on prom to attend some sort of academic triathlon. It was no wonder he'd done so well for himself.

It felt a bit like attending a bad high school reunion to purposefully meet with him again, especially when I was in such a tough spot. Attending my most recent *real* high school reunion—*was Elias even there?* I couldn't remember —had been nothing short of amazing. I'd just been promoted to Junior Booking Agent, we were happily married and had both managed to keep up our figures, and we'd begun considering selling our old house in order to relocate to the neighborhood I was already bragging about. It was the high school reunion of my dreams.

Everything about our lives was perfect, and I was still the person they all remembered. I'd lived up to my potential tenfold.

Of course, that was seven years ago, and look how much had changed.

Oh, how the mighty had fallen.

As I made my way toward the bar, I spotted Elias near the end, sipping on a beer and sorting through peanuts. I smiled as I neared him, and he spotted me, extending my hand.

"Hey. Good to see you again, man."

His handshake was firm, confident. So unlike how I remembered him. "It's good to see you, too. To be honest, I really didn't expect to hear from you."

I sat down on the barstool next to him. What I really wanted was a gin and tonic, but I went for a beer instead, noticing the three-dollar price difference. If I was somehow going to afford a place of my own, I'd need to pinch pennies harder than I ever had before.

"Yeah? Why's that?"

"I mean, we'd never really talked before. Truth be told, I wasn't sure you even remembered me. And I assumed you were pretty busy, being an agent and all. You know how it is."

"Yeah, well," I took a sip of the lukewarm beer, trying not to show my disgust as I looked at the bartender then back at Elias, "I had a meeting run late tonight, so I'm just going to hang around downtown for a bit before I head back to the—" I stopped short. "—back home. And I thought it would be nice to catch up."

He nodded. "Well, I'm glad you reached out. You're

right, it *is* nice. I can't tell you the last time I got together with a friend just to chill out and relax." He drained the last of his beer and set it on the counter, sliding it toward the bartender as he approached Elias with another. Elias looked back at me sheepishly, and I noticed the tips of his ears turning red. "Sorry, that probably makes me sound lame. I'm sure you have all sorts of friends you get to spend time with. This is probably just another Saturday night for you."

I was surprised by the vulnerability I heard in his voice, and I suspected, as his eyes shifted nervously waiting for me to respond, he hadn't meant to be so honest.

"Truth is, work keeps me so busy, I don't have much time for friends. This is the first Saturday I've taken off in a long time, and I called you because I thought if I didn't keep myself busy, I'd end up working anyway."

"Wow. Must be nice to have something you want to do even when you don't have to. You must really love it," he said, a question in his expression.

I thought about the words, weighing my response before I gave it. But I knew the truth. "No." I took another drink of my beer, no longer bothered by the inadequate level of chill. He scoffed, waiting for me to elaborate. "No, I really don't. I mean, don't get me wrong, it has its perks. I've gotten to meet some amazing people, travel quite a bit, and the pay is…nice."

"I'm waiting for the *not loving it* part," he said with a dry laugh as he popped a handful of peanuts in his mouth.

"It's great. I shouldn't complain. It's just…sometimes it's a lot. Everyone is trying to be something they're not, trying to impress someone, climb the ladder, you know? Sometimes it just gets exhausting."

"I hear ya," he said simply, not asking for further explanation. "Well, if it makes you feel any better, you're one of the first people I've talked to face-to-face in about two months. A ladder to climb, people to compete with, it all sounds pretty nice some days."

"What?" I couldn't help raising a brow. "You mean working for yourself isn't all it's cracked up to be?"

"Yeah, well, don't get me wrong. Going to work in my pajamas is pretty damn cool. But it doesn't mean I don't miss the interaction some." He laughed. "So, where are we on the pathetic scale? Two thirty-somethings at a bar alone on a Saturday night complaining about life."

"If either of us utters the words 'back in my day,' I think we've officially topped the charts." I tipped my beer toward him.

"Speaking of back in the day...I can't believe you and Addy are still a thing. We used to be so close, but you probably know that. We lost touch years ago... How is she? Do you two have any kids?"

A tinge of worry rang through me at the question, but when I looked his way, there was nothing sinister in his eyes. He was being casual, making conversation. But why was he so obsessed with my wife? And why did he care if we had kids? I forced the paranoid thoughts away. "Yeah, we have a daughter, Rory. Aurora, but Rory. She's fourteen."

"Wow, how wild is it that you're old enough to have a teenager? Jesus, I feel like we were just teenagers ourselves a few years ago." He ran a hand over his head, bewilderment registering on his face.

"Tell me about it," I said. "Sometimes it feels like yesterday, and sometimes it feels like a lifetime ago. Spend a few hours with a teenager, and you'll realize just how old you really are." I let out a chuckle then added, "Oh, but I guess I shouldn't assume you don't have kids yourself. Do you? Have kids or…a wife?"

"Nope," he said, popping the p before taking another sip of his beer. "There've been a few contenders here and there, you know? But no one ever, uh, no one ever…made the cut, I guess."

I drew in one side of my mouth with exaggerated sympathy. "Hey, that just means you have no one making sure you're home on a Saturday night. Total freedom, man." I couldn't even summon the mock excitement I needed to feel for him because I was too busy worrying if that would be my fate. I wanted someone to make sure I was home on Saturday nights. I wanted her to worry. I didn't want freedom if it meant losing her.

"Jesus, don't say it like you're a hostage." He patted my shoulder, a grin on his lips. "You don't have to pretend marriage isn't all it's cracked up to be. Food on the table every night, someone to watch stupid movies with, someone to take care of you when you're sick… Doesn't sound so bad to me…" He trailed off, his eyes glazing over. When he blinked, he looked as though he'd been lost. "I probably sound stupid. I'm sure you're like… itching for a break from normalcy, huh? You've been married since you were like twelve."

"Nineteen," I corrected, shaking my head. "And no, you

don't sound stupid. Not at all. Trust me. It's…the truth is, marriage isn't easy. Addy and I certainly aren't perfect. No marriage is. But I'd kill for a bit of normalcy right about now." I rapped my knuckles against the bar, looking at him out of the corner of my eye. "We're having some issues right now, so nothing's quite as normal as I'd like."

He looked genuinely downtrodden to hear the news. "Oh, no." As he lowered his head and clicked his tongue, he took another sip of his beer and another handful of peanuts before saying. "That's tough, man."

"Yeah, well, what can you do?" I asked, puffing my chest with a long exhale. When he didn't say anything, I heard myself going on. "It's life, you know? I'm not doing enough to make her happy because work has me so busy. But, it's like you said, we've been together for so long. Our marriage is the biggest constant in my life. I can't…" I trailed off, unable to finish the sentence for fear of breaking down.

"You can't lose her," he said, nodding as if he understood completely.

"I can't," I confirmed.

"So, don't," he said simply.

I raised my brows, leaning additional weight on the bar as I grew more comfortable. I'd never have guessed when I woke up this morning that I'd be ending my night spilling my guts to someone I hadn't seen since high school. "You say that like it's just that simple."

"Isn't it?" His blue eyes narrowed in the dimly lit bar.

"I wish it was. I've tried. Believe me I have. I'm doing everything I know to do."

"Everything like what?"

I opened my mouth then closed it again. "I don't want to bore you. You didn't come here to listen to me whine about my marriage. This was supposed to be fun."

"I'm having fun. Aren't you? I hate all that toxic masculinity bullshit. Who says two men can't discuss their problems. We're friends, aren't we?" He smiled at me, the pebble-sized teeth glinting in the glow of the red neon sign behind the bar.

I sucked in a breath. He was right. I did need to talk about what I was going through. Especially since Addy hadn't seemed interested in listening to my side of things. It would feel good to let it all out.

"Well, I guess it's just everyday stuff, you know? I work too much. We don't get to spend enough time together. We have different ideas about parenting now that Rory's getting older. And then her mom, oh my God, her mom... The woman practically lives at our house. She's always there. She'll just show up whenever she wants, and Addy is never bothered by it. Never mind that I pay for the house, that I stock the food in the fridge and..." I sighed. "It doesn't matter. None of it matters because I just want Addy back. I love her, and I'm willing to put up with all that extra crap to be with her."

"Have you told her that?"

"I have, but she doesn't want to hear it. She needs space. She wants me to get my own place, but I just don't think we're there yet."

"She kicked you out?" he asked, his brows knitting together.

"Yeah, three weeks ago. I thought it was just a tempo-rary thing, but she made it seem like it's going to be a lot more permanent than I realized. Seems like I don't get much say in the matter."

"So, what are you going to do?"

"I don't know. See, the trouble is..." I didn't want to admit the biggest piece of my vulnerability. "We can't really afford it. We've got an insane mortgage—"

"Green Hills..." He nodded, his lips pursed with understanding.

"Yeah, and we're paying for Rory to be in a private school there. And, I mean, I make great money, right? But she's a teacher; it's not like they're well paid. And rent here isn't cheap. Hell, it'd probably be cheaper for me to buy another house, truth be told. Plus, there's the whole issue of a lease. I don't want to be committed to anything when I'm hoping any day now she'll let me come home."

"That's rough, man. I get it."

I drained the rest of my beer and nodded as the bartender pointed in my direction. As he brought me a replacement, Elias said, "Well, hey, if you ever need a place to crash for a few days, my place is always open."

I jerked my head in his direction. "You serious?"

"Yeah," he said earnestly. "I mean, I know we don't know each other that well anymore, but it's better than rooming with a total stranger, isn't it? I have a spare bedroom in my apartment, and it's downtown so you'd be close to work. And you could stay for as long or short a time as you need. I'm a pretty easygoing roommate."

"Wow... I don't know what to say. Th-thanks. Um, what would you charge me?" I asked.

"Eh, you don't have to pay. Just get your food or whatever you need until you can get back on your feet."

"Why would you do that?" I couldn't help feeling almost skeptical at the generous offer.

"I'd hope someone would do the same for me if the situation were reversed," he said simply, shrugging one shoulder.

"I'm not a charity case... I'd want to pay you something."

"Suit yourself," he said with a tip of his head in my direction. "We'll work it out so you can pay me whatever you can afford. I get by okay. My business is doing well and my building's owned by a friend, so I live there for next to nothing. I don't have a lot of debt or anything. Just extra space, disposable income, and a lot of free time."

My jaw was slack as I stared at him. Was he serious? He didn't seem to be joking, but it was just too good to be true. "I don't know what to say, man. It would mean the world to me, honestly. It wouldn't need to be a permanent thing. Maybe just a few weeks, but it would really help me out with Addy. I don't have much stuff, so I wouldn't take up too much space, and I'm gone most of the day so you'd hardly notice me—"

"Hey," he cut me off, his hands up as if to proclaim his innocence, "you don't have to convince me. I've already offered you the room. It's yours if you want it."

"I'd owe you one," I said, extending my hand toward his.

"Don't mention it," he said. "So, when do you want to move in?"

# CHAPTER FOUR

I lugged the last box up the stairs to Elias' apartment. The building was sixteen stories of well-maintained brick and white, concrete-framed windows. The stairwell was open and airy, though chillingly quiet except for my heavy footsteps against the tile.

Elias' apartment was on the eighth floor, and the elevator was broken, so it had made for a very long day of moving in. My thighs burned as I reached my destination and walked inside. Elias was in his bedroom on a conference call with a client. He'd shown me around briefly and helped me carry the heavy stuff upstairs before setting to work, letting me know that I could interrupt him if I needed something, but only if it was absolutely urgent.

Compared to the dated outside, the inside was a breath of fresh air. The tall ceilings were lined with cherry-stained beams, and the walls boasted tall windows. The floors were a gray and white hardwood that matched the granite countertops and stainless steel appliances well.

It had two bedrooms, each with its own full bath and

decently sized closets. We'd agreed that I'd pay him a third of his monthly payment, as I was only using the one bedroom and didn't plan to stay for long. He'd insisted that I didn't have to pay anything, but it only seemed right. I'd wanted to pay half, but was thankful when he'd talked me down.

I shut the door to the apartment behind me and carried the last box of my things across the living room and into the bedroom. Elias had been using the room for storage, so I'd had to borrow our guest bedroom furniture from the house. Now, I would have the pleasure of getting everything set up.

I'd taken the day off, but I needed to get back to work tomorrow, so everything would need to get done that day. Over the next few hours, I positioned the furniture where I wanted it, moving everything across the floor cautiously so as not to scratch the pristine floors. Then, I put the bed frame together and laid the mattress and box spring on top. It was an old set from my parents, which meant the mattress had more lump than fluff, and it squeaked whenever anyone lay down on it, but it was better than sleeping on an air mattress on the floor. Besides, like I'd told Elias, it was only temporary.

I was going to convince Addy to let me come home.

This would work until then.

By the evening, the room was all set up, and I was placing the last of my clothes into drawers when I heard Elias' bedroom door open and close and his footsteps head in my direction. I glanced at the clock, realizing his workday must've been finished and wondering just how much I'd missed of mine. I hated skipping work on

Mondays, especially because our weekends were usually half days, which meant I already had a full day to catch up from on Monday mornings.

On the positive side of things, Addy had seemed impressed that I'd taken time off of work to get something done. When was the last time I'd done something similar for her? I should've taken off on a Friday and surprised her with a long weekend away.

If I ever got the chance again, that's what I would do.

The door to my bedroom opened, startling me and interrupting my thoughts. He looked around, eyeing the room peculiarly. I wondered why. I hadn't done anything to disrupt the space. I hadn't hung anything on the walls or scuffed up the floors.

"Almost done?" he asked, his gaze landing back on me.

"Yeah, almost." I held up the folded shirt in my hand before stuffing it into the drawer. "Everything okay?" Had he really walked in without knocking? This was my room now, wasn't it? The encounter felt strange to me, but I brushed it off.

"Yeah, I just finished up. I was going to go and grab some dinner. Do you want me to pick you up anything? I'm ordering from Etch."

"Oh, yeah," I said, standing up and walking across the room toward where my wallet lay. "Can you order me the lamb?"

"Sure thing. Want any apps? I'm going for the charcuterie board, if you want to share."

"You don't mind?"

"Not at all, roomie," he said with a chuckle. I handed him three twenty-dollar bills.

"I appreciate it." I'd been budgeting my meals lately, unless I was using the company card, but tonight I was exhausted and craving something that would send me to bed on a full stomach.

"Be back in a sec," he said, waving the bills over his head and shutting the door. I heard his footsteps growing farther away before listening as the door shut and I was left alone.

Quickly, I emptied the rest of the box and stood up, walking over to hang the last few shirts on hangers in the small, square closet on the far wall. I slid the door open, the stale air hitting me.

There were a few boxes in the far corner that Elias had said he was leaving. I shoved them toward the back of the closet and grabbed a few of the spare wire hangers he'd left me, hanging up my suits carefully.

I couldn't help dwelling on how bad my life had become as I made a mental note to purchase hangers that actually fit my suit jackets. Was this what rock bottom felt like? Broke, on the verge of divorce, going from having a house full of my possessions to a twelve-foot by twelve-foot room and only the mirage of enough closet space?

Once I'd maneuver the suits onto their hangers the best I could, I walked across the room, stacking the empty boxes together before I sank onto the bed.

*Creeeaaak.*

I groaned, closing my eyes as I focused on the *tick, tick, tick* of the overhead fan as it spun. *This is only temporary*, I repeated the mantra in my head. It would go back to normal. It wouldn't be this way forever…

When I opened my eyes again, I jolted. "What the—"

Elias was standing at the foot of the bed, a plastic sack in his hand. "Sorry," he said, though he didn't sound sorry at all. "I was just going to put your food on the nightstand for when you woke up."

I looked around the room, sitting up and rubbing my eyes. "I didn't mean to fall asleep."

"You were snoring. I didn't want to disturb you; it looked like you could use the rest." His blue eyes narrowed at me, and he placed the bag on the end of my bed, along with a few dollar bills and some change. I ran a hand over my face, letting out a yawn as I stretched.

"Man, I guess I am tired. I swear I just closed my eyes. Anyway, thanks for this." I slid the bag of food and the cash toward me, shoving the change into my pocket and opening the bag.

He remained still, watching me as I unloaded the bag. I got the strangest inclination he was waiting for a tip, the way a bellhop would linger once they'd delivered your bags. "Are you all settled in?"

"Mhm. Yeah, everything's unpacked. I didn't bring too much, luckily. But I managed to get it all unpacked and put away."

"Did you have enough closet space?" Somehow what should've felt like friendly conversation felt more like an inquisition.

"Yeah, it's perfect. You have a really nice place here."

His eyes traveled the room, as if he was realizing that for the first time. "It wasn't all that nice when I moved in, but I've had a lot of time to get it fixed the way I want it. My friend lets me do whatever I want here. I basically own the place."

"That's cool..." The tension was palatable. What was he waiting for?

"Are you sure you have enough closet space? I never have enough, and I have one more dresser than you. I could clear out a drawer if you need extra room."

The statement came across as strange, but he seemed earnest in the offer. "No, that's fine. I've got more than enough room here. I didn't bring too much, anyway."

"The laundry's downstairs, and there's always a wait. You may want to bring everything you have."

"Oh, no. I don't want to do that yet, not if I'm going to have to pack it all back up in a few weeks."

"You really think she'll let you back that soon?" he asked, running his hand along the footboard of the bed.

"I hope so..." I said, feeling disheartened by the skeptical look on his face. "Anyway, what did you get to eat? You didn't mention..."

His answer came in rapid-fire succession, all the sentences spilling out at once. "I got their lamb, too. I've never tried it, but it sounds amazing. Do you want to come watch TV? You're welcome to. I've got Netflix, Hulu, and HBO Max. I think I've got a coupon for a free Vudu movie around here somewhere, too..." He pointed toward the door. I desperately didn't want to go out there. I wanted to be alone. To eat in peace and go back to sleep. But he was staring at me so hopefully, I hated to say no. Besides, he'd done so much for me, it just felt wrong to say no to such a nice gesture.

"Yeah, sure," I said after a brief pause.

"Yeah?" His facial expression lit up. "Awesome. Okay, I'll get us some beers."

"Great. I'll meet you in there in just a minute."

He nodded, jogging out of the room gleefully, as if I was the first person he'd ever had over. Then again, maybe I was. He'd told me he didn't get much interaction with other people. Perhaps this was why.

After he'd shut the door, I stood from the bed, adjusted my clothing, and ran a hand through my unkempt hair. I lifted the to-go box from the comforter and headed into the living room, where Elias handed me a beer and settled in on the couch.

"You want to choose a show?"

"I couldn't even tell you what shows I like anymore," I said, twisting the top off my beer and taking a sip. "You choose." I felt the sadness swelling in my chest as I thought about the nights when Addy and I used to curl up on the couch and watch television together. When we used to save shows to watch for when we were together, so we could experience the twists and turns together.

The HBO Max logo filled the screen, and I watched as he chose a political show with Jeff Daniels. I zoned out most of the night, eating my to-go box of lamb in silence as Elias laughed and mumbled along with the characters beside me. I got the feeling he'd seen the show a few times before. He seemed so carefree it made me envious. What a simple existence he had.

When had my existence changed from simple to chaotic? Had I made the conscious choice? Had I decided to throw my life into disarray?

Not intentionally, maybe, but if you asked Addy, I believed she'd say yes.

"So, what's the deal with your marriage, anyway?" Elias asked, picking a piece of meat from his teeth. I was shocked by the candid question, but I tried not to show it.

"What do you mean?"

"Like...what happened? I know you've been together for so long. It must've been something big." I adjusted on the couch. It wasn't his business, but it would be rude to say so. "You don't have to tell me if you don't want to," he said begrudgingly. "I just thought...you know, you might want someone to talk to. Friends share things, right?"

"Yeah, it's not that. It's just that, well, I don't really know *what* happened. It was as if we were in two different marriages, and neither of us realized it." I tensed my jaw as I remembered Addy's words, thinking back over the fight—over all the fights—as he sat enthralled. His eyes were locked on me as if I were telling the most interesting story in the world. "You know, from my point of view, I thought things were fine. Truth be told, I never thought anything could tear us apart. We didn't cheat on each other, there was no huge fight or scandal. I don't know... She blames it on me, and I'm not saying I'm not to blame because I know I worked too much and I know I wasn't home enough, but we both agreed to it, right? We talked it all through, and she wanted me to take the promotion, chase my dream. I worked so hard for it, and now it's cost me everything." I shook my head, sighing heavily. "I get her point. I know I should've been there more often, but sometimes..."

I hesitated, the weight of my true fear on my tongue. "Sometimes what?" he prompted.

"Sometimes I just feel like she's using it as an excuse, and the truth is that she fell out of love with me somewhere along the way and is too afraid to tell me." My voice cracked as I finished the sentence, and I found myself no longer hungry. I'd never admitted that aloud, not even to myself, though the worry had been a bit more than a whisper in the back of my brain for some time.

"Nah... You don't mean that. If she loves you half as much as you love her, how could she fall out of love with you? I see that look in your eye when you talk about her, man. It's the real deal with you two. If she means that much to you, you have to fight for her. You have to. If you two can't work things out, what does that say for the rest of us?"

I smiled halfheartedly, my mind entirely elsewhere. Had Addy fallen out of love with me? I couldn't help worrying that was the case. And, if it was, no amount of fighting for our relationship was likely to help.

"What if you surprised her with something? Flowers, maybe? Or jewelry."

"Yeah, maybe." I agreed, fighting back bitter tears as I cleared my throat. "I'm sure I'll figure something out."

"You will. You'll be back together in no time." His tone was encouraging, and when I finally met his eye, I matched the easy smile he was giving me.

"Thanks. I hope so."

"And until then, you're welcome to stay as long as you need. It's nice having someone else around."

"I really appreciate that. I'm glad to be here."

"It's nice to be with a friend," he said, his words as serious as if they were a vow.

"It's nice to be with a friend," I repeated, though I silently prayed I wouldn't have to be there long. Elias was nice enough, but I wanted to go home. I wanted to be in my own space with my wife and child. I wanted to let my guard down a bit, and for whatever reason, with Elias, I couldn't quite do that.

# CHAPTER FIVE

Around two the next afternoon, my boss stuck his head inside my office, his face ashen, sweat gathered around his wrinkled brow.

"We need to talk," he said, entering without me welcoming him and taking a seat in front of my desk.

The words sent goose bumps along my arms, my throat suddenly dry. Why did the room feel smaller? "Okay."

He crossed one leg of his pleated pants over the other. "What I'm about to tell you, I need you to keep it silent until we can get the situation remedied."

"Of course." *Remedied* meaning we'd just lost a client. From the look on Stewart's face, it must've been a big one. "What happened?"

"We just found out we had a major hack in our network last night."

It took me a moment to process what he'd said. "We were hacked?"

"We don't know what information the hackers gained

access to before the system shut down. The IT department is looking into it. There's a good chance nothing was accessed, or maybe only a few nonconfidential things, but we should prepare ourselves for the worst, just in case."

"What would the worst be, Stewart?"

"Well, our clients' personal information may have been accessed. Home addresses, phone numbers, personal emails, legal names, banking information… We just really don't know."

My chest heaved with a panicked breath. "I don't understand. How did this even happen? We've never had anything like this happen before, have we?"

"No, never," he said adamantly, his heavy jowls quaking as he spoke. "It was all supposed to be very secure. From what I'm being told, the hacker was intelligent and determined to be able to break through the security we had in place. Oliver's a mess over it."

"Could it have been someone who works here? Or maybe a former client or someone we've turned down?"

"They're looking into all of that. I don't want anyone to get into a tizzy just yet. We should know more before we go home." He *tsked*. "I'm going to have to fire the entire IT department after this fiasco."

I rubbed my dry lips together, trying to remain calm. "Well, just keep me updated, will you? I don't want my clients hearing about this from anyone but me."

"No, of course not. Watch your email. I'll let you know as soon as I hear anything. Oh, and can you talk to your assistant and make sure he hasn't clicked on any strange links or visited unapproved websites? When we get to the bottom of this, there will be serious consequences for whoever is responsible." He groaned, rubbing his wrinkled forehead nervously. "That's why we put this information in the training. If people would listen around here..." He trailed off.

"I'll check with Gordon, but he's really good about that stuff. I can't see that he would've clicked anything he wasn't sure about. Gen Z-ers get that stuff. It's like ingrained in them."

He sighed, seeming weary. "Yes, well, check with him if you will anyway, and then wait for me to find something out before we take any further steps. Did you get the notification to change your passwords this morning?"

"Yeah, I did," I said, realization setting in. "I thought it was early to be doing that. It seems like we just changed last month. I guess it makes sense now."

"Yes, well...we wanted to be sure we'd covered our bases. You should change the passwords on any apps or accounts from your phone too, just to be safe. Anyway, I've got to go break the news to the rest of the team. I'll email you when I know more."

I nodded, turning back to my computer as he exited my office with just one more thing to worry about on top of my ever-growing pile. If any of my clients' information was obtained in the hack, there was a good chance I would lose them. And, if I lost enough, there was a good chance I'd lose my job. Without a job, I'd be unable to provide for my family or fix my marriage. It would take years to build up a strong client base at a new agency, supposing I could even find an open position. Without my income and with no savings to speak of, we'd lose the house within months. Addy and Rory would be forced to move in with Vivienne, and I'd have lost them for good.

After all, I'd staked our entire lives on this career. If I let Addy down by losing it, too, what reason would I find to keep her with me when she already had one foot out the door?

If I lost my job, I'd lose everything. Even if it wasn't my fault.

I cursed under my breath. Losing things I had no control of seemed to be a pattern lately.

———

WHEN I GOT HOME that evening, Elias was perched on the countertop with his legs crossed in front of him, scrolling on his phone with one hand while the other was shoved inside a white plastic sack. He lifted a piece of candy from the bag, a Swedish fish from the looks of it, and popped it into his mouth. I shut the door, though he barely looked up as I walked across the room.

"Hey," he called when I reached my door.

"Hey," I said, looking back at him.

"How was your day?"

"One headache after the other. How about yours?" I asked with a dry laugh.

"Did you not see me sitting here when you came in?"

"Yeah, I did."

"I thought you would've said hello at least," he said.

I furrowed my brow, shocked by his confrontational tone. "I didn't know if you were doing something for work. I didn't want to bother you." He reached into the sack, pulling a family-sized bag of Twizzlers out and onto his lap, and then taking one from the bag and biting the end off aggressively.

He stared at me for a long time, too long, and narrowed his gaze. Then, he let out a loud, obnoxious laugh. "I'm just teasing you. Do you want a Twizzler? I bought two bags."

I shook my head, both because I had no desire for the twisted, strawberry candy and because I was perpetually perplexed by him. "No, thanks."

"Not a candy guy? I should've guessed. You probably don't remember the last time you even ate sweets."

I cocked my head to the side.

"I just mean because you're in such good shape."

"Oh," I said with an overexaggerated nod. "Yeah, thanks. You're right, I'm not really a *sweets* kind of guy." I pushed the door open and walked inside, hoping to escape him. As I unbuttoned my shirt and pulled it off, the door popped open.

"Could you knock?" I asked heatedly, instantly regretting it.

He watched me, studying my expression and making me wonder if I'd crossed a line. His eyes turned icy as he stared at me, and I knew he was going to tell me to leave. Slowly, his lips upturned into a strange, cocky grin. "You really did have a rough day, didn't you?" He chewed the candy with his mouth open, red-tinged strings of saliva connecting his teeth.

"Sorry, yeah." I shook my head, trying to bring my anxiety down. Why was I taking my anger out on Elias, the one person in my life who didn't hate me at that moment? "We had some fires to put out at work, and it's been a day. But I didn't mean to snap."

"I'm sorry. I'm used to living alone and being able to walk anywhere. I should've knocked first. I'll try to do better."

"Don't worry about it. I overreacted." I pulled the shirt off my shoulders and grabbed a T-shirt from a drawer.

"You've kept yourself in great shape, Wes. You could probably give me a few pointers, hm? I don't ever go to the gym, but I know I should."

"Ah, I don't either," I lied. "I used to run, but I haven't in years. I haven't been to the gym in even longer."

He chomped on the Twizzler grasped in his fist. "Hm."

I picked up a folded pair of jeans, holding them awkwardly as I stared at him, waiting for him to take the hint. He didn't.

"So, what are you thinking for dinner tonight?"

"Actually, I'm going to try and grab Rory and take her to dinner."

"Rory?"

"My daughter."

"You have a daughter? You didn't mention it."

"I thought I did."

"Nope," he said, popping the last of the piece of candy in his mouth before grabbing another from the bag in his hand. His teeth were littered with bits of red.

"Ah, well, must've slipped my mind, then."

He sat down on the edge of the bed, and I groaned internally. "How old is she?"

Something about the question made my skin crawl. I turned away from him so he wouldn't see the irritated face I was sure I was making and headed into the bathroom, shutting the door firmly behind me before saying, "Did you say something?"

There was no reply as I pulled off my shoes and pants and hurriedly stepped into the jeans, keeping an eye on the lock at all times. After a few silent moments, I opened the door hesitantly. To my surprise and great relief, the room was empty. I walked back out, placing my clothes into the white mesh laundry bag lying in the corner. I grabbed my tennis shoes and slid them on, tucking my phone and wallet into my pocket and heading out the door.

Elias was nowhere to be seen, though I did quite a few double takes, half expecting to find him hiding behind the curtains or sitting atop the refrigerator. I eventually gave up, shouting, "See you later," and heading for the door.

Just as I reached it, my phone began to ring. I pulled it from my pocket, spying my boss's name on the screen.

"Hello?"

"Wes, hey. I stopped by your office to tell you the news, but I didn't realize you'd already headed home for the evening. I wanted to let you know what we've found out regarding the hack."

I backed up, resting my hip against the couch. His snide remark about me leaving the office at an earlier time hadn't gotten past me, but I let it go. "Yeah, definitely. I'm glad you called. What did you learn?"

He let out a sigh, and I immediately knew it wasn't as bad as I'd been fearing. "Well, the good news is the hack didn't make it to any client files or sensitive information from all we can tell. They were able to gain unauthorized access to our network, but it looks like the applications and confidential information remain unbreached. It's the strangest thing, almost like they accessed the network and then turned around and went home. So, that's the good news. The bad news is that we've had to fire Oliver."

The head of our IT department and one of the only people I genuinely liked that I worked with. To learn he had anything to do with the hack would've come as a total shock.

"Oh. Why? Was it his fault?"

"Well, I don't know that it was *entirely*, but it was certainly his job to prevent it. Thank heavens nothing consequential was accessed, but there have to be ramifications for something this serious. We're still in our early years here; we can't afford a scandal of such magnitude. There's banking information on those contracts, social security numbers, legal names, home addresses—it could've been apocalyptic if they'd been able to get any further."

I nodded, though he couldn't see me, and though I actually disagreed. Oliver was a good guy. I'd relied on him a few times when I'd lost a file or gotten myself locked out of the system. I hated to hear he was going down for something that hadn't actually caused any harm, but I understood the weight of the situation. A major crisis had been averted, I just wished Oliver wasn't being faulted for something he hadn't had control over.

"Didn't he prevent it from being as bad as it could've been, though?" I asked gently. "I mean, whatever system he had in place obviously managed to make sure they couldn't access anything too confidential."

Across the room, I saw Elias' bedroom door open, and he walked out, bag of Twizzlers still in one hand, a controller and headset in the other. I didn't meet his eyes as he walked across the room and sank into the couch behind me.

"Yes, well, that's the argument, but we pay good money to make sure they aren't able to hack into our systems *at all.* I can't really let it slide because they were only able to do it a little bit." He coughed into the phone, the sound growing quieter as I imagined he must be leaning away from the device to cough again. When he came back, he went on, "Look, I don't really understand most of the technical side of things, as you know, but I can't look weak right now. Someone didn't do their job, and it's Oliver who's in charge of making sure they *do* do their jobs. I can't just let this go." His voice was filled with agitation, as if he were trying to convince himself as well as me.

"I understand what you're saying. At the end of the day, you're the one who has to make the decision, and it's not one I envy." I sucked in a breath through my teeth, narrowing my gaze on the scratch in the hardwood between my feet. "I'm just glad it didn't end up as bad as we'd thought it could be."

"You and me both," he said with a heavy breath. "All right, well, I guess I'll see you in the morning, unless you're planning to come back in this evening."

"Yep, I'll see you in the morning." I ended the call, ignoring the question in his last statement and clicking the button on the side of my phone to lock it. Just as the screen went dark, a noise from the television caused me to jolt. I looked over at it, staring at a computer-engineered man dressed in combat gear on the screen.

Elias held a controller in his hands, his legs crossed in front of him as he stared at the screen. He grinned wildly, then looked at me, his eyes widening. "Sorry, did I interrupt you?" he asked, talking loudly over the noise.

"Nope, I was just finishing up," I called back, practically shouting though we were mere feet from each other.

"I thought so." He grabbed the remote control and muted the TV. "What was that about?"

"Nothing. Just a work fire," I said, tucking my phone into my pocket.

"No shit? The building? Or just a small one?"

It took me a moment to realize what he was asking. "Oh, shoot. No, neither. A figurative one. We thought we had a problem, but it's taken care of."

He let out a small laugh, and the amused look on his face as he chewed the candy in his mouth made me angrier than ever. Why was I feeling so frustrated with him? "You're so funny," he said, his tone chipper.

"Funny how?"

"So serious all the time." He put his arms up near his chest and folded them in as if he were a marching soldier as he imitated me, his lips drawn into a tight circle. *We thought we had a problem, but it's taken care of.*

I ran a thumb over my lips, not joining him in his laughter. If I didn't know he was my age, I could swear he was still a teenager sometimes. The childish way he acted irked me beyond belief. "Yeah, look...I've gotta get going. I'm not sure when I'll be back."

He laughed again, reaching out to stop me as I turned.

"Wait! Sorry, did I make you mad? I was just teasing. I didn't realize you were so sensitive."

"I'm not!"

"You're not mad, or you're not sensitive?"

"Either," I snapped. "It's just been a long day. I'm tired. I need to run a few errands."

He held his hands up in defeat. "No worries. I should've read the room better. I'm bad about that, sorry."

"It's fine. Honestly." I exhaled a calming breath. "Do you need anything while I'm out?"

I'd already turned away from him and was only half listening as I made my way toward the door, pulling my phone back from my pocket when he said, "What happened today?"

"Hm?" I spun back around, trying to keep my frustration hidden.

"That's the second or third time you've said you had a bad day. What happened?"

*None of your business.* It was no wonder he didn't have any friends. "Nothing really. I was just busy, that's all. I usually take a bit to decompress after work."

"Ah, okay. It just sounded like you might've needed someone to vent to. I don't mean to be nosy, but with Addy not around, I thought you might want someone new to talk to. I mean, we're friends, right? Friends vent to each other." He paused. "At least, that's what I've seen on TV. What do I know?"

"It's not that I don't want to talk to you. It's just work stuff—"

"You think I wouldn't understand?"

"No. It's just private. Not really my business to talk about." *Or yours to ask about.*

He was quiet for a moment, studying me carefully. Finally, he inhaled sharply, the amusement never leaving his eyes, and said, "You know, I had a girlfriend once who swore that there were no secrets that should be kept between best friends. She used to tell me that anything that happened between us was fair game to talk in depth about when it came to her and her best friend, Elizabeth."

I was silent, unsure what that had to do with what we were talking about at all, but he left me no time to guess as he went on.

"Do you believe that's true?"

"I don't know. I mean, I guess, yeah. Addy's like that with her mom. Vivienne. She tells her everything." I couldn't keep the bitterness from my tone. Though I'd never admit it to Addy, I'd always partially blame her mom for our separation. Part of that was due to the bitterness I felt about having no real relationship with my own family while her mother was her best friend. But a more significant part was just that I found it so unbelievably obnoxious that her mother was such a huge part of our life. Why should I be made to feel guilty about my job when her mother was practically her second job?

"So, why don't you think you can tell me the truth about what's going on? I'm your best friend, aren't I? We don't need any secrets between us, do we?"

His words interrupted my thoughts, and I stammered out an answer through a strangled scoff. "I-um, well, I-I mean, c'mon man... We hardly know each other. You're not my *best* friend. I'm not yours, either." I tried to say it lightly, but I watched the scar by his eyebrow draw down at the too-harsh words.

"You are," he said. "I mean, in terms of friends, you're basically the only one I have, which makes you the best, doesn't it? How many friends do you have?"

Truth was, none. Besides Addy, and I didn't have her anymore anyway. Other than that, I had clients and coworkers. None that I would consider friends or spend time with that I wasn't being paid for. I'd always been more of a lone wolf. Though I liked being a part of a crowd, the leader of a crowd even, I'd never been one to form close bonds with anyone. Until Addy came along, and even throughout our relationship, my solitary existence tended to cause more problems.

"I have friends," I said anyway. "And two brothers." Tom and Robbie, both years younger from my mother's second marriage, and both imbeciles. We hadn't spoken in years, but he didn't need to know that.

"None of them invited you to stay at their houses," he said simply.

I swallowed. "Yeah, well—"

"I mean, isn't that just the type of thing *best friends* do for each other?"

"Look, what do you want me to say, Elias? So I don't have any friends."

"You do. You have me."

"Okay, yeah. I have you. Fine."

"And I'm your best friend." He nodded encouragingly. My heart pounded, confusion and anger swarming through my mind at what had started out a strange conversation and, by an unimaginable feat, managed to only get stranger as it progressed.

"Yeah, sure. Whatever."

"So, why don't you trust me to know what happened to you at work? Or what that conversation was about? Did you do something illegal?" He seemed oddly fascinated by that possibility, his eyes lighting up and eyebrows dancing as he waited for me to answer.

"We had to fire a guy who really didn't deserve it, okay?" I said with more than a hint of exasperation. "Sometimes I just get really overwhelmed with how unfair life is."

"What did he do?" He held out a Twizzler for me, and this time I took it, just because I had no interest in fending him off any longer.

"Nothing. That's the worst part. He didn't do anything. Someone tried to hack into our network and failed, but because they made it past some sort of firewall or...I don't know. Something like that. Anyway, he's the head of IT, and someone had to take the fall, so they're firing him. And it just really sucks because he's a...he's a really good guy."

"I can see why that would upset you," he said sadly. "Surely there's something you can do. Aren't you a boss there?"

"Nah, I'm just an agent. I don't really have any pull. I mean, don't get me wrong, my boss talks to us and listens when necessary, but his mind's made up on this one."

"I mean, it's damn near impossible to have a completely impenetrable network, even with the very best cybersecurity system. Do you know what they were working with?"

"Oh, yeah. I forget this is what you do. I honestly have no idea."

"Do you want me to come in for a second opinion? Maybe I can help find the vulnerability, and then no one would need to get fired."

"No," I said too quickly. "That's not necessary. My boss probably wouldn't even like that I told you in the first place. I really appreciate you offering, though. Truly."

"It would be no trouble. You can just tell him you have a friend who works in tech and see if he'd be open to someone coming in and taking a look."

"Yeah," I said, because it was obviously going to turn into another fight if I didn't nip it in the bud right away. "Maybe. We'll see. Anyway, I need to get going, or I'm going to be late. Don't wait up, okay?"

"You got it," he said with a laugh, watching me as I walked toward the door. When I opened it, he unmuted the TV, and the blaring music returned in full force.

I hurried down the stairs, still shaking from the interaction.

What a weird little dude.

## CHAPTER SIX

I t took Rory nearly ten minutes to answer the door, still dressed in her clothes from school, when I showed up. If it wasn't for Vivienne's car in the drive, I would've thought they weren't home.

"Hey, kiddo. What took you so long? I tried to call your mom, but she's not answering her phone." I could swear her blonde hair had grown several inches since I'd seen her last, and her face looked different somehow, more mature. It had only been weeks, but it felt like years.

How much life had she lived without me?

"I was in my room," she said simply, as if that were enough explanation. She glanced down at her phone, her cheeks flushing pink as she displayed a wide grin. She tapped away at the screen, responding to whatever message had just come up.

"Where's your mom?" I asked, and when she didn't respond right away, I said it again. "Earth to Rory—is your mom home?"

She looked up at me as if she'd forgotten I was there.

"Sorry, yeah. She's out back with Vivi." The name Vivi-enne had requested each of her grandchildren call her. "Why? What are you doing here?"

"What do you mean what am I doing here? A dad can't come visit his favorite daughter?" I pulled her in for a hug, which she squirmed out of in a less playful manner than she once had.

"I'm your only daughter," she teased, her lips pursed. She looked so much like her mother when she made that face.

"Ahh, well that may be true, but it doesn't change the fact that I've missed you. How was school?"

"School was fine," she said with a long, drawn-out groan. "Why are you, like, interviewing me? What is this?" She waved her hands in the air dramatically, the bracelets on her wrists clinking together.

The attitude in her tone stung me. Had she not missed me at all? Was I so easy to live without? "What do you mean, interviewing you? I'm asking you about your life. I haven't seen you in weeks, kiddo."

"I'm not a kid, Dad," she whined. "Please stop calling me that."

"Okay, fine. I haven't seen you in weeks, Rory, and you can't even give me a hug? Haven't you missed me? You haven't called, and I know that thing is always attached to your palm. What is going on with you?"

"I've been busy, Dad. I have school and friends."

"You're never too busy for your dad." I teased. "Just, promise you'll call once or twice a week. Even just a text to let me know you're still alive...that you haven't forgotten who I am or run off and become some YouTube sensation."

Her face tinged scarlet. "Have you been watching my vlog?"

I laughed. "It's the only time I get to see you anymore."

Her hands went down to her sides defiantly. "Dad," she whined with an extra syllable on the a, "that's so embarrassing. Stay off my channel."

"I can't make any promises, but I can try to avoid watching if you'll give me a hug and promise to call."

"Fine." She leaned in for a halfhearted hug to appease me, one arm still at her side.

"What's Vivi doing here anyway?"

"She's liv—" She stopped short, pulling away from me with a petrified look on her face.

"What is it?"

"She didn't tell you?" she asked quietly.

"Tell me what?"

"Dad, Vivi moved in last week. She's staying here permanently."

"Perma—no." I shook my head. "What about her condo? She can't be living here permanently. What will happen when I move back in?"

Rory raised her eyebrows as if to say, *not my problem*, but instead chose, "No idea." She glanced down as her phone buzzed again, tapping away at the screen as I shut the door behind me. "Do you want me to tell her you're here, or…" She trailed off, not bothering to look up at me.

"No, that's okay. I'll talk to her. You said she's out back?"

"Mhm." She waved her hand in the general direction of

the backyard, walking away from me and down the hall toward her room.

"I'll come find you before I leave. I want to catch up."

She didn't respond, and I heard her door shut a few moments later, leaving me in the quiet of the house alone. I walked down the hall and into the kitchen, noticing the pristine sink as I moved past it. If I needed it, that was further proof that Vivienne was, in fact, living there.

When I'd been at home, weekday evenings were always filled with piled-up dishes and rushing through dinner. Vivienne was ever the homemaker and, as she said all too often, she could never dream of sitting down in a messy house.

As I made my way through the kitchen, then the dining room and toward the back door, I spied Addy's phone lying on the baker's rack where the bowl of car keys and other random odds and ends sat. When I'd been living here, she didn't go anywhere without her phone.

Why had she changed for her mom, but not me?

I knew I had so much to be blamed for in the downfall of our marriage, but, at least to myself, I would not accept sole responsibility.

Without another glance at her phone, I knocked on the screen door that led outside, feeling stupid as soon as I'd done it, but it had worked. Addy's and Vivienne's heads cocked back in unison, looking to seek out the disturbance. They were sitting in the wrought iron patio chairs on the paved patio in the backyard. The built-in fire pit was between them, though it had no fire in it.

I stuck my head out the door, waving my hand awkwardly. "Sorry to interrupt."

"Wes, what are you doing here? Is everything okay?" Addy asked, putting a hand up to shield her eyes from the sun.

"Yeah, everything's fine. Sorry. I didn't realize you had company. Hello, Vivienne."

"Hello, Wesley. How are things?"

"Things are fine," I said stiffly, spying my favorite mug in her hand. *#1 Dad*, it read. Why hadn't I taken that with me? "Can I borrow Addy for just a sec?"

She didn't answer, looking at Addy, who stood from the chair with a sigh and headed in my direction. She was still dressed from work, her hair tied back the way it often was when she had to focus.

She pulled the door back and stepped inside, and I watched Vivienne lift up the plum Kindle that had been lying next to her chair before I shut the door.

Addy studied me, her face pale. "What's wrong?"

"Nothing. I told you. I just wanted to talk."

"You could've called."

"You don't answer when I call," I told her.

"You ever think maybe there's a reason for that?"

"What if there'd been an accident, Addy? Even if you're mad at me, you still need to take my calls. We can be adults about this, can't we?"

"Was there an accident?" she asked skeptically.

"No, there wasn't, but there could've been."

"I've told you I need space, Wes, but you keep calling and stopping by. How is that giving me space?"

I inhaled, taking a half step back to regroup. I didn't want to fight with her. The conversation had to be redirected. "You told me you were going to talk to Rory about coming to stay with me. Did you do that?"

"Not yet, no. I wanted to give you a few days to get things figured out and yourself settled in first."

I wasn't sure I wanted to ask the next question, nor did I know how to bring it up, so I just spat out, "Speaking of *settling in,* did you move your mother in here without consulting me?"

She sighed, glancing down the hall toward Rory's room. "Is that what she told you?"

"Yeah, she did. The question is why would she have to tell me? Why wouldn't you? Why would you move her in here in the first place? Is that how little faith you have in me? In us?"

"Hold on," she said, holding both hands up. "Calm down. I didn't move my mother in. She's staying here with me while we deal with our stuff, but she's not moving her things in or anything like that."

"But why? Why would you do that? You know how she feels about me—"

She looked at me as though I were crazy. "Wes, you're her son-in-law, the father of her grandchild. She loves you."

I scoffed. "Yeah, okay, like she loves people who say 'Happy holidays' instead of Merry Christmas."

She pursed her lips. "She does love you, Wes. And, the truth is, I could use the help. I don't understand why you insist on vilifying her. You don't want us to move in with her, which I understand, but she can still help me in other ways, and she wants to do that. More than that, I *need* her to. She's not judging. She's not trying to manipulate me

69

one way or another. Believe it or not, she doesn't want us to get divorced. She just wants what's best for us all, and she's trying to do what she can to help. Since Dad died and she sold the house, she's all cooped up in that condo with nothing to do; this is as good for me as it is for her."

"And what happens when I come back? Hm? *If* I come back. Is she going to leave then? Because I'm not going to be the one to have that awkward conversation." I huffed, then grew quiet as the realization swept over me. "Unless she doesn't expect that to be an issue. Does she think I'm not coming back?" She hesitated, and my stomach lurched. "Do you think I'm not coming back?"

"I don't know what to think, Wes. We're still trying to figure everything out. That's the point of all of this, isn't it? To get some clarity."

"I don't know, Addy. Why don't you tell me what the point of it is, since you're the one orchestrating everything. Pulling us all around like puppets on strings and pretending you're the victim in the entire situation."

Her jaw dropped. I'd crossed a line. I watched her steely eyes narrow at me. "I'm not the victim here, Wes, and I'm not pretending to be. If anyone is a victim, it's Rory, whose entire world has been torn apart and who has no idea what her future looks like. She doesn't need us in the dining room fighting right now. We need to be united."

"That's all I want," I said angrily. "I don't want her hurt. I don't want her future uncertain. If it were up to me, I'd be right back here and things would be back to normal."

"But I don't want normal. Don't you get that? Normal

wasn't good anymore. Normal wasn't working for anyone."

"Normal wasn't working for you, Addy. Speak for yourself here."

"Fine," she agreed. "Normal wasn't working for me, then. Normal doesn't work for me anymore."

"So, what? That's just it? Decision made? Were you even going to tell me you'd moved her in here?"

She pressed her tongue onto her top teeth, pausing briefly before answering. "I didn't want it to be a whole thing. She knows it isn't permanent."

"Is it not?" It was the first she'd said to lead me to believe she might think I could move back in.

"It..." She stopped, chewing her lip before her hands raised into an exaggerated shrug. "None of this is permanent, is it? If you move back in, she'll move out. If you don't, we all move out. We can't keep this house for much longer if we aren't together."

I felt the words take the breath from my lungs.

"Is that what you want? Be honest, Addy. Do you want this to be the end of...of everything? Of us? Do you want me to move on? Is that what this is? Are you trying to let me down easy? Because if that's what this is, I'd rather you just tell me now."

"That's not what this is. I love you, Wes. When I make a decision, decide what I want, I will tell you. I won't string you along either way. I see that you're attempting to be better, okay? I do. I'm just trying to work through my feelings about everything."

I reached for her hands, and to my surprise, she let me take them, holding them in the space between us. "Well, I want you to do that. I do. I want you to take whatever time you need. But I also need you to communicate with me. Not every day, fine. But we're still married. I need to know what's happening with our daughter. Our house. You have to keep me in the loop."

She nodded, staring at me. "I know. I'm sorry." Her gaze fell to the floor momentarily and then came back to me. I could still get lost in her eyes, even in the middle of a fight. "I should've told you about Mom, but it's really not a big deal. I don't want you to make it into something it's not. I was struggling to get everything done, and she offered to help. Simple as that."

"Why wouldn't you let me help?"

A skeptical brow raised. "Since when do you have the time?"

"Since now," I told her. "Seriously. What do you need?"

"House stuff, mostly. I'm trying and failing to keep up with it all. I needed help with laundry, dishes. Rory had soccer, and I had work, and the house was falling apart, so Mom stepped up."

"You should've given me a chance."

I watched a muscle in her jaw twitch as she fought to keep her expression calm. "You had a chance, Wes. When you lived here."

"Well, I'm asking for another one."

She seemed to think for a minute before shaking her head, her hands going up. "No. No, that's too complicated. I don't need anything complicated right now. I need simple. The goal of this whole thing is to give us space apart. Time to clear our heads."

"Yes, space. I get it. So, why don't you let me come over

when you are out? Let me take Rory to practice or let me clean the house while you're doing that. Your mom shouldn't have to move in to help out when I'm perfectly capable."

"Since when are you perfectly capable? How are you going to get the time off?"

"I'm here now, aren't I?"

Her face softened, the skin around her eyes wrinkling subtly as she squinted at me. "Why are you here, Wes?"

"I wanted to see Rory. I told you to let me know about getting her to visit my new place, and you haven't contacted me."

"It hasn't even been three days since you told me you were moving into a place. I assumed you'd need weeks to get there and get settled."

"No, I'm in. I'm settled."

There was a wave of appreciation and shock on her face. Her jaw dropped open as if she was going to say something and then closed quickly. "You are?"

"Yeah, I'm all moved in."

"How is that possible? You've already been approved, paid the deposit, everything? You just borrowed the bed and picked up your things yesterday. I thought you'd just found a place. I assumed you'd have to wait a few weeks to hear if you were approved. I was trying to figure out where you were going to keep everything, honestly, but I've been trying not to pry."

"Pry away, Addy. I don't mind. I didn't even have to apply. I moved in with someone."

"You wh—"

"A man. A friend," I added quickly. "The one I told you

I met at the store the other day, actually. Do you remember a kid named Elias from high school?" His last name suddenly escaped me.

"Elias..." she said the name slowly, letting it weigh on her tongue as her gaze scanned the room. Suddenly, her eyes grew wide. "You don't mean *Elias Munn?*"

"Yes, that's it! Munn. Elias Munn."

Her face lit up, and she clasped her hands over her mouth. "Oh, of course I remember Elias! Oh my goodness, he was always such a little sweetheart. How is he? Bless him... I had no idea he was still around here. I haven't heard from him in years." She tapped a finger against her lips, lost in thought, then she eyed me. "Wait a minute, you mean you moved in with Elias Munn?"

"I sure did," I said. "Is that a bad thing?"

She hesitated, studying my face. "No, I guess not. Don't you think it's a little weird, though?"

I shook my head. "He offered me the room for dirt cheap. He's a little odd, but nothing I can't handle."

"No, it's not that. I just... Wow, I just didn't expect it. It was so sweet of him to offer you a room. I can't believe that." She shook her head in shock. "I mean, I can, I guess. He always was a sweet kid. A bit misunderstood... A bit odd. I just never thought he'd be someone you'd want to live with. I can't honestly picture you with a roommate at all."

"I'm not marrying him, Addy. I'm just living with him for a little while until we can work through our stuff."

"Hey, I'm not complaining. I think it's great. Really." She nodded affirmatively. "Did you remember who he was? I knew you said you didn't get his name that first day. You didn't exactly run in the same circles when we were in school. I'm surprised you even remember him now."

"I still don't, really. I know he was the one who won that, like...multiplication olympics."

She giggled. "Science decathlon, yeah. They were the state champs, from what I remember."

"Yeah, right. He was younger than us, right?"

"Yeah, by a few years, I think." She twisted her mouth in thought.

"Right, yeah. I mean, once he gave me his name, I realized who he was. I didn't know him well, though. I would've never remembered him on my own."

"And he has the space for you? Does he have his own place?"

"Yeah, an apartment downtown. He has a spare bedroom."

Her brows shot up. "And that's where you're expecting Rory to stay? With you and Elias Munn?"

"Don't say it like that. It's a nice place. A really nice place, actually. Right across from the river. She can come over, and the two of us can go out to eat or shop or whatever she wants downtown, and then she can stay overnight... I'll give her the bed and crash on the couch. I just want to see her."

"Will Elias be okay with that? Doesn't he have a family? Plans? He's not going to want you bringing a bunch of people over."

My mouth dropped open slightly. Why did it still feel like it wasn't enough for her? No matter what I did... "Rory isn't a bunch of people. And he's already told me how lonely he is. He doesn't have a family. And I haven't run it by him yet, but I know he'll be okay with it. He's a really cool guy, actually." I hoped she didn't catch the bluff in my voice. Elias was far from *really cool*, but I didn't have a choice. If I wanted to see my daughter, I had to make the best of it.

"I think it's great that you're staying with him. It sounds like it'll be good for both of you. I just don't know how comfortable Rory will be staying with you and some strange guy."

"Look," I said, fighting to keep the frustration at bay, "I don't know what you want me to do, Addy. We can't exactly afford for me to rent my own apartment. Elias is hardly charging me anything, which is great because *hardly anything* is all we have. You won't let her stay with me in a motel, so I get a place, and now that's not good enough for you either. Short of letting me come home, what else is there to do? If you have the budget for my own place stashed away, please do let me know."

She chewed her bottom lip, running her fingers across the bridge of her nose. Finally, her hands went up in defeat. "You're right, Wes. I'm not being fair. I'm so sorry. This is all just new to me."

"I know what you're saying, but think of how new it is for me. At least you're still in a familiar place. This is *all* new to me. Literally all."

She nodded. "I appreciate you getting a place so quickly. I know it isn't easy for you, and I know how much you must miss her. How did you manage to get moved in so quickly anyway?"

"I took yesterday off."

She did a double take, her head jerking backward. "I'm sorry. You did what?"

"I took the day off to get moved in so Rory could visit sooner. If I'd tried to work through the evenings, it would've taken me all week to unpack and get moved in. You knew I was coming to get my stuff while you were at work."

She blinked slowly, processing what I was telling her. "Yeah, I thought you were just going in a few hours late. You mean you took *all* of yesterday off?"

I tried to hide the triumphant smile I felt playing on my lips. "Yeah, I took the whole day. I wanted to get it done. I knew how important it was to you."

"So, wait. You're saying you're off right now when it's only," she glanced at the clock on the wall, "five thirty. And you also took yesterday off."

"Yeah, that's right."

"Who are you and what have you done with my husband?" she joked, watching me closely as if she truly suspected I were an imposter. I'd obviously impressed her, and I saw my chance to make a move.

"I'm still me, but I'm trying to be better. I heard what you were saying, Addy. I heard you, and I'm trying to make the changes to prove to you how serious I am about you. About us. I know I wasn't doing everything I needed to for you. For Rory. I know you weren't happy here, and I'm sorry it took you kicking me out for me to finally listen to you. I love you so much, and I'm going to do whatever it takes to prove that to you. And I mean now. Not in a month, not next week, now. I'm going to be better for you because that's who you need. You need the best version of me, and I'm going to give you that."

I swallowed, breathlessly staring at her as I waited for her response. It was the best speech I'd ever given, and I hadn't rehearsed a moment of it. She stared at me, unblinking, as she processed what I'd said with a soft gaze.

"I love you, too, Wes. And that truly does mean so much to me. Thank you for...for hearing me. I'm really impressed and appreciative of what you're doing."

I wanted her to say I should move back in, that I'd done enough. That I'd proven how serious I was, but I couldn't ask. I couldn't press. She'd given me an inch, and I couldn't ask for more. "I'm glad to hear it. And I really am sorry for stopping in unannounced."

"I should've answered your calls. I know I should have. It's just so hard to talk to you. It just...it makes me sad, Wes." A hint of tears glimmered in her eyes, and I watched her blink them away quickly, clearing her throat.

"Talking to you is still the highlight of my day," I told her honestly.

She didn't respond right away, instead taking a deep breath, seeming to collect herself as she brushed away a stray tear. "I will tell Mom she doesn't have to stay here anymore if you want to start taking Rory to her soccer practice on Thursdays."

"Yes, I would love to," I said quickly, practically before she'd finished the sentence.

She grinned, almost laughing. "And I stay late at the school on Wednesdays to grade papers, so if you want to come over on Wednesday nights, you can have dinner with her."

"Yes. Done."

"You'll have to cook."

"I can do that."

"I can't guarantee that she'll want to spend time with you. She's always YouTubing or FaceTiming, and there's this new boy that she likes—"

*"A boy?"* The warmth of the moment had disappeared at once. Since when was my daughter interested in boys? Seriously, anyway.

She grinned, shaking her head. "My point is, my time with her is mostly her in her room, but I can tell her how important it is to you. I know she misses you."

"I miss her," I said. "I miss her mom, too."

She cocked her head to the side, staring at me with a dreamy expression. I'd almost sold her, I could tell. I was close to closing the deal. "And as for staying all night," she interrupted my thoughts, "I'll talk to her about spending every other weekend there with you. She wants to be with her friends more than anything, Wes, and I don't want to take that away from her right now. I know she's having a hard time with this, and I don't want to take away anything that's helping to keep her mind off of things for a bit."

"I don't want that either. I just miss her."

"I know," she said, patting my chest cautiously. I lifted my hand to cup hers, and to my surprise, she didn't pull it away. I studied her face, my eyes drifting back and forth between hers. I wanted to kiss her, to smell her hair, her

79

skin, to feel her warmth, but I couldn't push it. If I went too far, she'd back up farther. I had to bide my time.

"Thank you for that," I said, releasing her hand. "I really appreciate it."

"It'll be good for her." She gave a stiff, serious nod. "And it'll give me time to get things done around here, too."

"And I'll do whatever I can on Wednesdays, too. Dishes, laundry, whatever."

"Don't flake out on me, Wes. That's all I'm asking of you. If you say you can be here and then you don't show up or cancel at the last minute, it's going to leave me in a real bind. Mom can't get here that quickly to take her to practice, and I don't like Rory taking Ubers alone."

"I'll be here," I vowed, and I knew then and there, I'd move heaven and earth to make sure that could happen.

"And Wednesdays, you need to be here in time to cook. I could have her cook, I guess, but—"

"I said I'll be here." It was my turn to reach out, touching her arm gently. "I mean it. I'm making a commitment to you. I won't let you down."

It hit me then, just how often I had let her down. How often I'd broken her heart. I could see that in her expression. Just how often I'd been the source of her disappointment. Never again, I vowed silently to her. I wouldn't do it. Couldn't. I'd never again be the reason she hurt.

Even if it killed me.

# CHAPTER SEVEN

After I left the house—Addy's house, our house, I wasn't sure what to call it anymore—I drove around town, taking back roads I hadn't taken in years as they were never the fastest route to wherever I was going and, for years, I'd always been in a hurry.

Addy had promised to talk to her mom. Our routine was going to start immediately, and I'd be working my way back into her life—and eventually her heart—in no time.

I was in no rush to make it back to the apartment, so I drove the curved roads slowly, turning onto streets I didn't know and making circles around blocks I had no need to be on. How long had it been since I'd driven just for the fun of it?

How long had it been since I'd had the time?

I wasn't sure, but the truth was, I hadn't had the time for anything in such a long time. Not for my marriage, that was for certain. Not for my daughter. Not for my friends. Not for my family. Not even for myself.

How sad was it that now that I had nothing left, I suddenly found the will to give myself the time I needed? I could've done it all along, but nothing had been that important to me.

What did that say about who I was as a person? What did that say about what kind of man, what kind of father, what kind of husband I'd been?

It made me sick to think about all I'd missed out on because of work. Work that would've been just fine to wait another day, another hour, another week even.

Now, I was just a man living alone, with a strange roommate and a distant, growing daughter, and a wife who'd had her heart broken one too many times.

It was maddening what I'd let happen to my life and how hard I'd need to fight now to get back what I'd once taken for granted.

I desperately didn't want to go back to the apartment, not if it meant having another awkward conversation with Elias, but as the sun set and the sky turned dark, I knew I didn't have a choice.

The next day was Wednesday, and I'd be ending it by having dinner with my daughter, plus dealing with whatever fire was surely waiting for me at work, so I needed to get home and rested. I could only hope that Elias had already made it to bed by the time I arrived.

Sure enough, though, when I made it home, I could hear the music through the walls as I climbed the stairs and approached the door. I put the key in the lock and turned it carefully. Elias hadn't moved from his spot on the couch, controller in hand.

"Oh, you guys are dead," Elias said, paying me no

attention as I made my way into the living room. If I were an intruder, he'd never have known I was there. I made my way across the room, hoping to go unnoticed, but just as I got behind him, he called out.

"Hey, there's pizza here if you want some." He gestured to the half-eaten box of meat lover's pizza on the coffee table in front of him. "Help yourself."

"Thanks," I said, planning to turn down the offer, but at that exact moment, my stomach growled and I realized I hadn't actually eaten anything since lunch. I sat down on the couch next to him, reaching for a slice. It was cold, but it settled in my stomach instantly, the nourishment much needed.

"Did you get your errand taken care of?" he asked, not taking his eyes off the screen as his character battled his way through a body-clad field, with bullets flying in every direction. What exactly was he playing?

"Yep. It's all handled." I was suddenly self-conscious, worried he was going to tease me about being too serious.

"Want to play?" he asked, noticing me zoning into the game out of the corner of his eye.

"Oh, no, thanks though. What is this game anyway?"

"Only the greatest game in the history of the world. *War Demons: Battle of the Great Unknown*," he told me, his voice mystical as he waved his free hand in the air like a magician.

There was a dash of pizza sauce on the corner of his mouth that had been drying for quite some time from the looks of it, but I didn't bother pointing it out. "Hm, nice."

"Have you ever played?"

"Nah, I was never that into video games."

He paused the game suddenly. "What?"

"Yeah. It's just not my thing." I took another bite of the pizza, hoping to end the conversation. Taking the hint, he pressed play again, resuming the game as he laughed dryly, almost like a hacking cough.

"We'll change that, Wes. If you live with me long enough, you'll be just as good at this game as I am, and I'm a level eighty-seven warlord slayer. That's almost as high as it gets."

I stared at the screen, his words haunting me as I listened to him clicking away on his controller.

*I won't be here that long, Elias. I promise you I won't.*

I thought it to myself, rather than saying it aloud, because it was more of a cry than a statement. I couldn't stay there long enough to learn that. I wasn't sure I'd survive it.

# CHAPTER EIGHT

The next day, when I left the house, Elias' bedroom door was closed, a sure sign that he'd already begun his workday. All the better for me, honestly. I made my coffee in peace, no need to carry on futile conversation, and cooked some bacon. Then, for good measure, I left him a plate in the fridge, the strips wrapped in a paper towel in case he smelled it cooking and wanted some.

I was glad for the peace and quiet, truth be told. Elias had found a way to fill every moment of my silence at home with endless questions and conversation.

It was just another thing I missed about Addy. She knew when I needed my space. When I'd mentally checked out and just needed to sit in silence. Elias didn't seem to have that ability or care.

After breakfast, I washed the pan and placed it back into the cabinet—I was practicing being a better husband, even if it was just for Elias—grabbed my to-go mug, keys, and phone, and headed out the door.

When I walked into work, my skin grew cold.

*What the...*

I stared at the sight, though none of it made sense. Why was he there?

No.

No.

What the hell was he doing there?

I stormed through the buzzing lobby, bursting into my boss's office without knocking, something I'd never do ordinarily.

"Wes!" Stewart said gleefully, mid-laugh at a joke I hadn't heard. "Come in, come in." He waved me over to his desk, but I was too busy staring at Elias to pay him any attention.

"Hey, buddy," Elias said. "I'll have to tell you what your boss just said. You didn't tell me he was so funny. Has he heard it?"

Stewart chuckled loudly. "I don't think so."

Elias pointed a finger-gun at me. "Have you heard the one about the two sailors who take an RV trip?"

I shook my head. "I-I'm sorry. What am I missing? What are you doing here?"

"You were holding out on me," Stewart said, still chuckling to himself. "You didn't tell me you had an in with someone in IT."

"I didn't know that would matter..." I trailed off, still trying to make sense of it all. Was I in a dream? Had I not actually woken up that morning?

"And not just *in* IT, but a leader in the field. Elias here is one of the leading cybersecurity specialists in the South. Did you know that?" he asked, patting Elias' shoulder.

"I..." I shook my head, still not comprehending what was happening.

"When you told me what was going on, I just couldn't not get involved. Not when my friend's company needed me so badly. Cybersecurity is my passion, bud. How could I not step in and come to the rescue when you so obviously needed me?" He put a hand on my shoulder, a twinkle in his eye as he glared at me.

"Elias here was just telling me he was going to offer our company a free IT checkup. He thinks he can figure out where the hackers gained access and set us up with a VNB—"

"VPN," Elias corrected.

"Right, right. VPN."

"We didn't already have one of those?"

"Well..." Stewart rambled off, shaking his head. "I'm really not sure. He's checking now. You know how I am with these things. Give me an opportunity, and I'll make a sale. Give me a computer, and I'll make a mistake." He chuckled under his breath, but Elias joined him in an uproarious fit of laughter.

"That was a good one, sir. You're killing me." He looked at me, his arms folded over his stomach as he laughed. "How do you work with this guy?"

I stared at them both in utter horror, feeling like I'd woken up in another universe. Bizarre didn't begin to cover it. How had my awkward roommate suddenly become the life of the party? And why was he here? I'd told him to stay out of it. Why wasn't Stewart mad?

When the laughter faded out, obviously drained quicker by my lacking sense of humor, Stewart cleared his throat, pulling himself up in his chair. "Well, anyway, Elias here is going to fix us right up. And we have you to thank for it."

"Yes, but I didn't ask him to come—"

"Oh, buddy!" Elias' hand was back on my shoulder, his grip too tight. "You know you didn't have to ask. That's what I was telling Stewart before you got here. I know you were feeling shy about asking for a favor, but it's really no trouble at all. I'm happy to help. After all, what are friends for?"

He smiled at me, his pebble-teeth poking out from behind his lips, and I felt a sickly feeling wash over me. Why was he here? What did he want? Why couldn't he just take no for an answer?

"Stewart, look… All due respect here, I just don't think that it's really the best idea in the world for us to be mixing our personal lives with work. Isn't that what we've always said? It's why we don't have Christmas parties or company picnics. It's why you don't like our families to visit the office. You've always said it winds up causing more trouble than it's worth."

He grumbled, his wild, gray eyebrows dropping down to a furrowed expression. "Now, this is business, Wes. We're a business, and your friend is here doing his business and helping ours—"

"I know, but—"

"Which is *very* nice of him, especially in these *hard economic times*, and given what we had to fork over yesterday to find out the extent of the breach and what we were looking at to apply even more security to our servers. Wherever we can save a penny, well I'm certainly willing to do it, aren't you? Why snub our noses at such a lovely gift, Wes? Especially from your friend." He gave me a stern look.

"Oh, don't mind him, Stewart. He's just being modest. That's what I like to call him. Ole shy, modest, serious Wes," Elias said, patting me on the head playfully. He winked at me. "Relax and let me do my job. I've cleared my day for this." He cracked his knuckles. "Elias is the name, destroyin' malware is the game."

With that, they broke out into another chorus of laughter. I groaned internally, forcing a smile when Elias winked at me.

"Elias, listen, it's really sweet of you to do this, but honestly, you don't have to—"

"I know I don't have to, silly goose. I want to. I like helping my friends, Wes. I like helping you." As he said it, even with the warm smile on his face, a sort of darkness swept over his eyes, and I felt a chill trail down my spine.

Something wasn't right about Elias.

Something wasn't right at all.

# CHAPTER NINE

I spent all day in the office, which was rare for me. Usually, I searched for any excuse I could find to get out and about with clients, visiting venues and traveling the city. That day, though, you couldn't have pried me from my chair.

I watched Elias move through the office, laughing and chatting with each of my coworkers as he worked at their station. It didn't sit right with me. How was he able to charm them so easily? Why did they seem to like him, some of them even more than they liked me? How had he gotten rid of the eerie personality that was so front and center back home?

For someone who mostly worked from home by choice, I found it bizarre that he'd chosen to come to my place of work without being asked. I found it even more bizarre that he hadn't asked me before he did it. His words about wanting to climb a ladder and missing human connection rang in my ears. Surely he wasn't going to try and get Oliver's job... The thought was terrifying. I couldn't handle him twenty-four hours a day. I wouldn't survive it.

Perhaps the most bizarre part was how easily he seemed to be getting along with each of my coworkers. Before, he'd told me that he had trouble talking to people. That he didn't always fit in, and I thought I'd seen that firsthand. But here, he was fitting in just fine. He was like an entirely different person.

Stewart couldn't seem to get enough of him, our receptionist had hand-delivered him two coffees since he'd arrived, and everywhere he went, people seemed to follow, watching him work as if it were the most fascinating thing. Every so often, I'd hear bursts of laughter through the glass of my office, an unfamiliar sound in our usually quiet and busy workspace. Why was Stewart allowing this? Just to save a buck?

I couldn't explain the anger I felt toward Elias, but it seemed to be growing by the minute. As I watched him sit at a desk across the lobby, eyes focused on the computer with a goofy grin on his pale face, two of my coworkers leaned down over him, as if what he was doing were the most fascinating thing in the world. I'd never seen anyone react to Oliver that way.

Just then, my door opened slowly, and I jerked my head in that direction. Oliver stood in the doorway, a fist raised as he knocked on it while at the same time swinging it open. He ran a hand through his frizzy, black hair, his freckled face even paler than usual, somehow.

"Hey, man," I said, standing up and extending a hand for him to shake. "I'm sorry to hear about yesterday. How bad was it?"

"Hey, thanks," he said, shaking my hand back. "Well, obviously, we realized we were vastly unprotected. Nothing like that has ever happened, you know? We never really expected that we'd be the victims of such a large attack. We were protected from the basics, but this was... an attempt at a massive scale." He sighed, shaking his head. "But, it's handled and, luckily, thanks to you, I'm not going to be losing my job, so those are two giant-ass positives." He tucked his hands into his pockets with a chuckle.

"Thanks to me?"

"Thanks to you and your buddy, yeah," he said, nodding in Elias' direction. We watched him through the glass of my office.

"Oh, no, that wasn't... I mean..." I had no idea what I was trying to say.

"No, no. Don't be modest. Elias told Stewart he'd only do it if he didn't fire me. Since I don't know him from Adam, I can only assume that came from you. Stewart called me an hour ago and told me I had my job back." My jaw dropped at the news, and I looked at him, utterly shocked by what he'd said.

"Are you serious?"

"Yeah," he pointed back and forth between Elias and me, "you mean you didn't know?"

"No, I had no idea. I mean, I'd told him I was upset that you were going to get fired when I didn't think it was your fault, but I didn't even know he was coming in."

"Well, hell of a friend you've got there, bud. I owe you both a beer..." He chuckled. "Or ten."

"Yeah."

Now, guilt ate at me as I began to wonder if I'd judged Elias too harshly. Was he truly just a bit awkward? Did he only want to be my friend?

Oliver sighed beside me and held out his hand again. "Anyway, I should get back to work, since I actually have a job to return to, but I just wanted to come by and say thanks again. You saved my ass."

"My pleasure," I told him, still in complete shock at what had transpired. With that, he walked back out the door, leaving me to watch Elias closely.

I couldn't quite figure him out, and I felt like there was something to that. Maybe there wasn't anything wrong with him after all; perhaps there was something wrong with me instead.

What had happened to me so that I thought anything good that could happen to me must be malicious? Why couldn't I accept the kindness I was being given? Why couldn't I have a conversation with a friend without being confrontational?

I wanted the answers to each question, because, even knowing what I knew, even hearing what I'd heard, I still had this unmistakable feeling as I stared at my roommate across the office.

Deep down, even as he smiled and laughed with my coworkers—people he hadn't known until a few hours ago, people he shouldn't have known at all—I couldn't quiet the whispering voice in my head repeating on a steady loop.

*Run.*

# CHAPTER TEN

When it was time for Elias to work on my computer, he walked in my office, a giant grin on his face.

"Man, it's no wonder you like working so much. Your coworkers are great."

"They are?"

"Yeah, SarahBeth was telling me all about the Bake-Off she had with her grandma's book club last week. Have you heard that one?"

I shook my head. "Sarah who?"

"SarahBeth," he said, pointing out the window toward the dark-haired receptionist I had only spoken to in passing. "The one who sits next to Lenora."

"No, I haven't heard it." In truth, I didn't know Lenora either. Receptionists and interns came and went so quickly, I'd stopped bothering to learn their names a long time ago.

"It's a hoot. You should ask her about it," he said,

wiggling his fingers as if he were on a keyboard already. "Okay, let me work my magic." His head bobbed back and forth. "First trick, you out of your seat." He threw both hands over his shoulders animatedly, grinning wildly. "Ope, here we go."

As I stood, he took my seat in a hurry, and I pulled a chair up so I could watch him work. "What are you doing exactly?"

"Oh, just your basic tune-up," he said. "We'll start with a backup." He turned to me, wagging a finger in my face dramatically. "It's like I was telling Stewart, you always, always want to back up. You guys should be backing up more often, really. Then we'll run a few software and operating system updates, check the hard drive for errors, run a malware scan, do a deep dive searching for any corrupted files, get rid of any lagging programs, do a quick defrag, and do a backup again. Bada bing bada boom, you're back to work without knowing what hit you." He dusted his hands in the air.

"Well, I don't understand most of what you just said, but thank you for doing this. And for putting in a good word for Oliver. I know he appreciates it."

"*No prob, Bob.* Any friend of yours is a friend of mine." He winked at me again. "Okay, now let me get on with it. Stewart promised me the last piece of pecan pie in the break room when I'm done."

"There's pecan pie in the break room?"

He looked at me and laughed quietly, as if I was joking. "You've really got to talk to your coworkers more." He turned back around, looking at the computer. "Oh, first things first." He whipped open my desk drawer, riffling through it.

"What are you looking for?"

"This," he said, pulling out a stack of sticky notes, swiping the top one off, and slapping it on top of the monitor.

"Of course. And why did you do that?"

He removed it, tapping his finger on the webcam. "Why did I do that?" he asked himself, rolling his eyes playfully. "Webcam, Wes. Need I say more?" He chuckled under his breath, placed the sticky note back over the webcam, and got to work.

As I turned and looked out over into the lobby, I noticed each computer now had a bright sticky note slapped upside down over their own cameras, and I couldn't help smiling at myself.

What a *weird* little dude.

---

ELIAS LEFT the office that afternoon just before three, pecan pie on a paper plate, and I headed out shortly after him. The entire office kept the sticky notes up long after he had left, and I found myself being talked to by coworkers I'd never spoken with before, all thanks to him.

As off as I found the entire thing, I couldn't say I wasn't thankful for what he'd done. Stewart was absolutely delighted by it all. He couldn't stop thanking me, and Oliver, of course, was the most thankful of all.

As I left, I made the decision to do something nice for

Elias to show him how appreciative I was, as I worried I hadn't been as kind as I should've been when he'd caught me so off guard that morning.

So, I wanted to surprise him with something small but thoughtful, but all that I knew about him was that he liked computers, video games, beer, and food. Of those items, beer and food were the only things I could entertain the idea of being an expert on. I didn't know what the protocol was for one guy to buy his friend a gift, but it was important to me that I show him I appreciated what he'd done, even if I questioned his motives.

I stopped by one of my favorite restaurants downtown and grabbed us two of their best burgers with a side of house fries that I'd placed an order for an hour before. Then, I picked up an extra case of beer and headed back across town toward the apartment.

When I got home, I heard his shower going. He was singing loudly to a song in what sounded like Spanish, and I hurriedly set out dinner and beers, changed out of my work clothes, and sat down on the couch. I was still there when he emerged from the bathroom a few minutes later, hair wet and dressed in his pajama bottoms and a T-shirt.

He looked over what I'd done and grinned slowly, as if he were beginning to understand. "What is all this?"

I looked over my shoulder at him then turned around, resting my arm on the back of the couch. "I wanted to say thanks for what you did today."

"You already said thanks."

"Well, I wanted to do something else."

"Oh," he waved me off, "you didn't need to do that. I told you, it's what friends are for."

"I know, but it's important to me that I thank you. You really saved the day today. Not only with Stewart, but for Oliver. It was...it was really nice. I got short with you yesterday after work, and I didn't deserve a favor after the way I acted. But Oliver really did deserve to keep his job, so thank you for helping him out."

"I told you, I was happy to help. Now, if your boss's car goes out, you'll have to make a new friend. But as far as computers go, I'm your guy."

I laughed along with him, to which he seemed pleased.

"Seriously, you've done so much for me, Elias. And...I haven't been as good a friend as I want to be. I'm sorry for that."

"You don't need to apologize," he said, running a hand over his hair. "Seriously. We're good. I like helping you." There it was again, that phrase that sent chills down my spine this morning. Still, it didn't sit right with me. "So, what did you get us?"

"Burgers and fries from Jack Brown's. I picked up some extra beer, too. And I was thinking you could teach me how to play that video game you were playing last night."

"Oh, that?" he asked, though he obviously couldn't hide his excitement. "I don't know... Are you sure you're really into that sort of thing? I thought you didn't like video games."

"Yeah," I said, trying to sound much more *into that sort of thing* than I was. "But I thought you were going to try to change my mind."

"I'm happy to teach you, Wes, but you have to respect the game. It's serious business, not some little kiddy game like you might think."

"I didn't think it was a kid's game, Elias. There were bodies all over the—" *Shit.*

*Kid's game.*

*Kid.*

*My kid.*

I was supposed to be having dinner with my kid.

"What is it?" He read my panicked expression.

"I'm so sorry." I closed my to-go box and leapt from the couch, glancing at the watch on my wrist as I rushed to the counter and picked up my keys and phone. "I can't…" I checked the time again. I had half an hour to get across town before it would be time for dinner to be ready. *Shit. Shit. Shit.* "I'm so sorry, Elias. I have to go."

"Go? Go where? I thought we were going to play the game? What, are you worried about getting your ass kicked?" he taunted, but it was futile as I was already making my way toward the door.

"I know. I completely forgot I have a thing. I'm supposed to be having dinner with my daughter, and I swore to my wife I wouldn't miss it or be late, which is exactly what's happening right now. *Where are my keys?*" I shouted to no one in particular.

"Your hand." He pointed to the keys held in my palm.

I looked at them. "Right. Shoot. Sorry. Okay. I have to go. God, I'm so sorry. You just…enjoy the meal. I'll be back late, but I promise I'll make it up to you. You can teach me the game the first free night I have. I swear. Tomorrow. *No, tomorrow's soccer.* Someday. Friday. Someday. I'll take it seriously! Okay. Okay, I've gotta go." I shut the door like a gust of wind, leaving Elias standing alone and looking utterly confused as I rushed down the stairs, not realizing I hadn't even slipped on shoes until I was already in the parking garage.

# CHAPTER ELEVEN

I made it to the house half an hour late, relieved to see that Addy wasn't home. She wasn't supposed to be, I knew. That was the whole point. But the entire way over, I'd driven with a nagging sense of dread that said I'd be met in the driveway by my wife, tapping the toe of her polished high heel into the concrete.

My anxiety hadn't totally subsided, though, as I knew Rory could still let her mom know I'd failed the very first test. It wasn't my fault, but that didn't matter. It never mattered.

The day's events had been so exhausting and distracting, it was a miracle I'd remembered at all, but I could never tell Addy that. As I stepped out of the car, I couldn't get the devastated look on Elias' face as I walked out of the apartment from my head. Every time I closed my eyes, there it was. I couldn't bear to add Addy's disappointment to the mix.

I grabbed my bag of dirty laundry that had been in my trunk from the motel and the to-go box from the front seat and headed up the sidewalk toward the house. The door was locked when I arrived, and though I'd promised Addy I'd treat the house with respect and not walk in or use my key rather than knock and be let in, I decided to make an exception at that point. If I could just walk in, there was a good chance Rory wouldn't even know I hadn't made it there on time.

So, for the first time in weeks, I used the key on my keychain to let myself inside the house that had once been mine, but now felt strange and foreign, and made my way into the kitchen.

Rory was sitting at the island, a bag of carrots open in front of her, holding her phone with one hand. When I entered the room, she glanced up just briefly enough to say, "You're late."

*Well, shit.* "Yeah, I know. I'm sorry. I got stuck in traffic," I lied, immediately feeling guilty about it. But then, it was for a good cause. I'd been given my shot, and I couldn't afford to blow it. In front of Rory, in the center of the island, were the flowers I'd had sent to Addy as a thank you after she'd agreed to our latest arrangement. Though she wasn't the kind of person who would do something so cruel as to throw them out, seeing them there in one of our best vases had me awestruck. Perhaps this was a sign. Maybe she was trying to tell me there was still a reason to have hope. I fought back the smile growing on my lips and looked back at my daughter. "I stopped and grabbed you some dinner from Jack Brown's." I held out my to-go box to her as a peace offering. She eyed it carefully.

"Where's yours?"

"I got hungry on the way over." Another lie as the grumble in my stomach let me know almost instantly, but this one I felt decidedly less guilty for.

She popped a baby carrot in her mouth and laid her phone facedown on the island, folding her hands in front of her as she surveyed me carefully.

"Mom says we're supposed to talk or...something."

I nodded, my voice shaking as I answered. "Yeah. I would like that."

She crossed one leg over the other, reaching for the burger. She opened the box and picked it up with careful hands. Once, she'd have dug straight into her food without regard for how it would look or the mess it would make. Now, I watched her careful moves, the way she dabbed her cheeks after taking the tiniest bite. She had changed so much. No longer was she the carefree young girl I'd loved so much. She'd become a self-conscious teenager without me realizing it, and it made a pit in my stomach at thinking of how much I'd missed, even when I'd still been there.

"So... What do you want to talk about?" she asked once she'd finished the bite and dusted her hands over the box.

I pulled out the barstool sitting next to her and dragged it toward me, giving her some space as I sat down. "Well, why don't you tell me how school's going?"

"School's school," she said with a shrug, tearing a piece of lettuce from the burger and tossing it into her mouth. "Nothing too exciting."

"How was your beach trip? Your mom said you went with Tessa, right?"

"Yeah, it was fun," she said. We sat quietly for a

moment, and she added, "I was hoping it would be warmer while we were there, but it was still nice. We had dinner on their boat one night and saw dolphins. Her dad got a picture of us in front of them."

"Wow. That sounds like a lot of fun."

"Yeah..." She tore another piece of lettuce free, rolling it between her fingers.

I ran a hand over my mouth, trying to think of anything else to say. The lulls in our conversation had already grown uncomfortable. "Hey, do you remember a few years ago when we went to the beach for summer vacation and we found those baby jellyfish on the sand?"

"No," she said simply, her expression sad. She laid the lettuce down.

"You were young..." I tried to think back. It didn't seem that long ago, but perhaps it was. "Seven or eight maybe. There were so many of them. Just these...jelly blobs on the sand. You had a fit when we told you you couldn't bring them home with us." I thought back, trying so desperately to recall the memory. "Maybe you were even younger than that."

"I don't remember," she said firmly. Drawn from my thoughts, I looked up at her. Her face was stone, serious and vaguely empty. Had I done something to upset her?

"It was a long time ago," I conceded. "I wouldn't expect you to, I guess. We had plenty of other good vacations, didn't we?"

"Mom says we went to Disney when I was three. I don't remember that either."

I twisted my mouth in thought. "Yeah, she's right. We

did. And we went on the cruise with Vivi and Paw when you were...eleven or twelve?"

She nodded. "I was eleven. I remember that one, of course. My first time leaving the country." She paused. "Speaking of vacations and leaving the country, did Mom get a chance to talk to you about this summer?"

I furrowed my brow, trying to remember. "I don't think so. What's this summer?"

"Tessa's parents invited me to summer with them in Venice. Mom said she would have to talk to you, but it would be so cool, Dad. I've always wanted to go there. And it would be educational, too. Don't worry. Tessa's mom always makes sure we're doing educational stuff, even when it's boring."

"Wait, slow down... *Venice?* As in Italy?"

"Yeah, where else?" she asked with a nervous laugh.

I hesitated, the hopeful look on her face a knife in my heart. "I...I don't know, honey. I'm not sure how I feel about you leaving the country without me or your mom with you."

Her face fell into an exaggerated frown, her mouth open. "But how is that fair? When are we ever going to leave the country again? When are you ever going to have the time or money to take us to Italy? Don't you want me to experience other cultures? Don't you want me to try new things?"

"Of course I do. You know I do. But what if you were hurt over there? What if something happened?"

"Nothing will happen. Tessa's parents are really responsible. They'll take care of us. We'll stay with them the whole time. It'll be such a good experience. Tessa's dad says he thinks kids who don't leave the country at least once a year for their childhood end up stunted culturally. Tessa goes three or four times a year. We've only left one time, and a tourist-filled port in Cozumel doesn't even really count!"

"Sweetheart, I'm not trying to hurt you or upset you, or...*stunt you culturally.* I just want what's best for you."

She slammed her fist down on the countertop. "Italy is what's best for me."

"We knew when we moved here that there would be kids who could afford to do more than we can. We talked about that. We don't have the money most of the families around here have. You know that. But your mom and I do all we can for you."

"But not this? Why? Why won't you let me go? It won't cost you anything. Tessa's parents already said they'd pay for everything. You just have to say yes."

"It's not about the money, Rory. It's about your safety, and sending you to a country we don't know a lot about with people we don't really know doesn't feel safe to me."

"Is it my fault you don't know a lot about Italy? Or that you don't know Tessa's parents? *I* know them." She slapped her hand on her chest. "Don't you trust me to know I'll be safe?"

"You're just a kid, Rory. You can't possibly understand what I'm—"

"Fine," she cut me off, tears swimming in her eyes. "I don't know why you even brought me here to this stupid place. To this stupid house with these stupid people. You took me away from my friends, away from my team, and now you and mom are splitting up and you won't let me do anything I want to do! *It's so unfair!"* she screamed.

"Hang on, now," I said, trying to calm her sobbing. I stood up and walked toward her, but she pushed off the chair and stepped backward. "Look, sweetheart, I just—"

"Don't. I don't want to talk anymore, Dad. I'm done talking. Just forget it. Forget everything." With that, she picked up her phone and stormed past me, leaving me with her mostly untouched dinner, unadulterated guilt, and the sounds of her sobbing and moaning from behind her bedroom door.

When Addy arrived home a few hours later, I was still in the kitchen. The dishwasher had been emptied and reloaded, and I'd washed and folded two loads of laundry for her. I was cleaning the stove when she walked in, dark spots across her teal shirt from the incoming rain she'd been caught in.

She took in the sight of me cleaning and smiled. "Wow. The house looks great."

"Well, I had a lot of time on my hands."

She raised a brow, slipping off her jacket. "You did?"

"Rory has decided I'm the worst parent in the universe, and she never wants to talk to me again." I tried to say it with the humor it deserved, but I couldn't deny the way it stung to recall her screaming it through her bedroom door when I'd tried to talk to her.

"Oh, that's you today, huh? I guess I got demoted." She shook her head. "What happened?"

I scratched my head. "Italy happened."

She rolled her head back, letting out a groan that looked identical to the one Rory had released just hours before. "I told her I was going to talk to you about it. She wasn't supposed to do this tonight. I'm sorry."

"She completely blindsided me. I didn't know what to say."

"What *did* you say?"

"I mumbled something about not wanting her to get hurt, and…honestly, the rest is a blur."

She chuckled, folding her jacket over her arm. "She'll be fine. I'll talk to her."

"You are saying no, though, right? I mean, it's ridiculous. She can't just…go to Italy. How long is she even wanting to stay there?"

"The entire summer," Addy said. "Doug and Caity have a villa in Venice with a full-time staff. Apparently Doug is good friends with a soccer coach for their women's league. He's already promised Rory an introduction."

"An introduct— *She's fourteen years old!*" I exploded.

"Hey, I'm on your side of this, remember? I told her I thought she was too young, but I wanted to talk to you before we made a decision."

"But the decision is still no, whether we talk or not, right? You can't honestly be considering letting her traipse around the world like she's nineteen and taking a year abroad."

"Well, she wouldn't exactly be *traipsing* the world, Wes. She'd be with her best friend and her best friend's parents. I like Doug and Caity. Tessa has been a good friend to Rory."

"So what are you saying? You actually want her to go?"

"I don't know, Wes." She reached up, placing her jacket on the coat rack that hung from the wall and setting her purse on the sofa table in the hall before walking past me into the kitchen and filling the coffee pot with water. Coffee was her go-to whenever she was stressed. There were many years during the beginning of our relationship when coffee was one of the only things we could afford. We'd practically been living on it for quite a while. I couldn't smell it now without thinking of her. She scooped the coffee into the filter before saying anything else. "I agree with you. It's too much, but we can't hold her back from everything. We knew what we were signing up for when we moved here. We knew what we'd be getting into. These are her friends, and she doesn't want to be the only one not getting to do all of the stuff they all get to do."

"You're saying you think she should go?" I asked again, because she really hadn't given me an answer.

"I'm saying I want her to get to experience whatever opportunities she has. Does it absolutely terrify me? One thousand percent. But does that mean I want to say no? Also yes. Am I going to? I don't know if I can, Wes. How can we surround her with these people and tell her she can't participate in anything they get to do. It's why things were just so much simpler before. It's complicated here, and it's only getting more complicated as she gets older."

I watched her tuck a blonde curl behind her ear as she pulled down two mugs without asking if I wanted one. Of course, she didn't need to ask. I would stay until she kicked me out if it were up to me.

"How did you leave it? When you talked to her."

"I told her I didn't know if it was safe and that I'd talk to you, and then she stormed out and it sounded like there was an exorcism in there for most of the evening," I said plainly.

"About as well as could be expected then, hm?" she asked with a dry laugh.

"About as well as could be expected." I chuckled under my breath, my chest tight. I couldn't help still feeling wound up over the incident.

She poured the coffee before the pot was fully brewed, putting two spoonfuls of stevia in hers and a bit of powdered creamer in mine before handing me the coffee mug. She smiled at me and tilted hers toward mine. "Another problem for another day."

I tapped mine against hers and lifted the mug to my lips. Her calmness was contagious, and I let it pass through me.

Once she'd taken the first sip, she looked around again. "It really does look great in here. You worked hard."

"Thanks," I said halfheartedly. "I did as much as I could. Laundry's folded and put away. I've got a load of my clothes in the dryer now that I'm going to wait for if that's okay. I fixed the cabinet door, too." The one I was supposed to fix over a year ago but kept forgetting to do. Neither of us mentioned that, but I knew it was there in the air between us. I was trying to do better.

I was trying.

She nodded. "I really appreciate it."

"Thank you for keeping the flowers, by the way." I gestured toward the vase in the center of the island.

Her cheeks grew pink as she looked toward them. "Of course, Wes. It was…really thoughtful of you to do that. You didn't have to."

"I know I didn't, but I wanted to. I wish I'd brought you flowers more often…before."

Her smile was sad and wistful, her eyes distant. "They are beautiful. You really surprised me. I love y—" She stopped herself, looking down. "Them. I love them."

I swallowed, trying to pretend the correction of what she'd been intending to say hadn't stung. *Don't you still love me?* Nevertheless, I recovered quickly, changing the subject. "How was work?"

She appeared relieved to be talking about something else. "Oh, you know… It is what it is."

I leaned against the counter. I'd never heard Addy talk about her work that way. She loved being a teacher. It had always brought her such joy. Was she really so miserable there now?

"Did you have a rough day?"

She seemed taken aback by the question. "No worse than usual, I guess. I love what I do, don't get me wrong. I love my kids. I love teaching. But…" She sighed. "Forget it. I don't want to complain. I'm blessed to be doing what I love."

"Don't do that… I really want to know. You aren't complaining. Talk to me."

She smiled and took a seat at the island, a weight visibly lifted from her shoulders as I sat across from her. "It's not about the money for me. You know that. It's never been about that for me."

"I know." And I did. Addy had never cared about money. She was the type of person who'd donate everything we had—in the form of school supplies, clothing, shoes, and even lunch money—to the kids in her class who didn't have enough. She kept boxes of snacks in her desk drawers for the children who hadn't gotten breakfast at home and, every Christmas at the old school, she'd organize a toy and coat drive to make sure no child went without. She was a selfless person whose entire heart went into helping the children in our community. Part of me had always wondered if our contrasting ideals when it came to money and wealth would be the thing to drive us apart—the jury was still out on that.

"But sometimes," she went on, interrupting my thoughts, "when I see kids driving cars that cost more than I make in a year or tossing out sweatshirts that cost more than my monthly salary because they got a snag in them, it's just really hard, you know? That's not what I want Rory to think life is like. I'm glad she's getting a good education, don't get me wrong. I'm very thankful she's able to go to the Academy, but sometimes I just wonder if the things she's learning from her peers are worth the sacrifice for her education. The other day she asked me why we couldn't just hire a maid or two to help us out instead of having Mom stay with us. She's starting to think these things are normal, and I don't want that for her. The kids in this neighborhood, they just don't live in the real world, Wes. They live in the world of lavish vacations, private jets, live-in staff, and two-thousand-dollar outfits. We just aren't those people, and it's really starting to get to Rory. I don't know how to make her understand that it's a good thing, that there's nothing wrong with the way we live and that we're actually very well-off compared to the way you and I grew up. I feel like we're failing her."

"We aren't failing her," I argued, though I had no concrete proof to the contrary. "We love her."

"Yeah," she said sadly. "That we do…"

"If you want to leave, if you want to go back to our old neighborhood, to your old job, let's just do it. Let's just go."

She gave me a wary look. "My position's been filled—"

"So, we'll find you a new position."

"And we'd have to sell the house first—"

"We'd have offers by tomorrow."

She smiled at me, reaching her hand across the counter to clasp mine where it rested. She squeezed my hand gently, brushing her fingers across mine and, for just a moment, I felt her lose herself in my gaze, just as I was doing in hers. *There we were.* The people I remembered: The couple from prom night. From graduation. The husband and wife bringing their baby into the world, their entire lives in front of them. The couple blissfully in love not so long ago.

She let out a long exhale. "Let's not talk about that. Let's just be here, okay? I'm exhausted. I don't want to think anymore."

"Okay," I said, buzzing from her touch. I didn't want the moment to end.

It was as if nothing and everything had changed all at once. The moment was reminiscent of our early years together, when we could find the spare time to just sit and talk for as long as we had.

Every evening, we'd spent so much time together. Just being in each other's presence. Talking, laughing, existing.

It felt like it had been so long since that had happened, and I suppose it had.

"How was your day?" she asked, interrupting my thoughts and pulling her hand back slowly, almost regrettably.

"Pretty great, actually," I told her, thinking back over the day.

"Oh, yeah? What happened?"

Just as I was about to tell her, the dryer buzzed, letting me know my clothes were done. We looked down the hall in unison, toward the laundry room.

I looked at my coffee, still steaming hot. "That'll be my clothes. Should I...get going?"

She seemed to think for a moment, her lips pressed into a thin line. "Do you want to?"

My head shook before I'd meant for it to, giving my answer for me. "I never want to leave you, Addy."

Her eyes glimmered, and I watched as they traveled to my lips and back up to meet my gaze. She leaned in slightly, without warning, and for just a brief moment, I thought she was going to kiss me. My chest swelled, my heart thumping loudly in preparation.

All too quickly, she leaned back, seeming to realize what was happening, but the warmth of her smile never left her lips. Finally, she let out a breath through her nose and lifted her mug to her mouth. "Stay for a while. I'm in no hurry."

And so, I stayed.

# CHAPTER TWELVE

When I arrived home that night, it was late, and I practically floated into the apartment, still high on my time with my wife. Nothing had happened in particular, but she'd let me stay, we'd had coffee, we'd laughed. She'd helped me fold my clothes, we'd talked more about our days, and, for the first time in so long, we hadn't fought about a single thing.

I was a changed man. Forever in awe of what could happen when I put my mind to it. I'd said I would fix things, and tonight I'd seen in Addy's eyes the first signs that I was actually doing it.

Elias was already in bed, and I set my bag of laundry down and walked across the quiet apartment, making my way to the refrigerator in search of a bottle of water to take to bed with me. I wasn't really tired, my body buzzing with adrenaline, but I knew I needed to at least lie down and attempt to sleep before work in the morning.

I grabbed a bottle of water and shut the fridge,

glancing at the open trash can as I noticed the to-go box from Elias' dinner sitting there, the untouched burger on top. I leaned down closer, trying to be sure I was seeing correctly.

"You're back." The voice behind me caused me to jolt, letting out a strained squeal. I looked over my shoulder to where Elias stood, just behind me, outside of his bedroom door.

I put a hand to my chest, releasing a shaky breath. "Jesus. I didn't hear you coming." He was eerily quiet. Was that on purpose? I'd never met anyone who moved so stealthily.

"I heard the door open, and I wanted to be sure it was you. You can never be too careful."

Oh, great. Creepy Elias was back. I smiled, though he didn't reciprocate. "Well, I'm sorry. I didn't mean to disturb you. I figured you were already in bed."

"I was waiting up to make sure you got home okay."

My shoulders fell. "Oh. Elias, you didn't need to do that. I'm an adult. I can take care of myself." I tried to say it lightly. I knew he was disappointed that I'd had to ditch him.

"Did you not like your burger?" I asked, jutting a thumb toward the trash. "I guess I should've asked what you preferred, but I didn't want to ruin the surprise."

"Oh, it wasn't that. I just don't eat meat."

I let what he'd said process. "What?"

"Yeah, I'm a vegetarian, so I ate the fries, but I couldn't eat the burger. I really appreciate the gesture, though."

"But…" I felt like I was going mad. "You ate lamb with

me the other night. And meat lover's pizza. How can you be a vegetarian?"

"I've always been a vegetarian," he said simply. "You must be confused."

"No, I'm not. I watched you."

"You couldn't have," he said forcefully, though there was still a light tone to his carefree voice. "I don't eat meat. Not since I was a teenager. It's murder."

I shook my head. It couldn't be true. I'd watched him eat the lamb. I knew he'd eaten the pizza. Still, it didn't seem worth arguing with him. "Okay, I must just be confused then."

"Must be," he said. "No worries. Are we still on to play the game tomorrow? I dug my old controller out of the closet for you to use."

I winced. "Well, not tomorrow. I have to take my daughter to soccer practice, but Friday for sure, okay? I'm looking forward to it."

His face went stony, and I watched him blink once. Twice. "Okay."

"Is that all right?"

"Yeah, just squeeze me in whenever you have the time," came the clipped reply.

"It's not like that. I'm really looking forward to it, honestly. I just need to help my wife with my daughter's schedule. At the end of the day, I still need to make her happy, so I can move back home."

"To Addy."

"Yes, to Addy."

He nodded again, then turned abruptly and walked

away, disappearing into his room and shutting the door without another word.

"Good night, then," I said under my breath sarcastically.

As much as Elias perplexed me, he'd done me several huge favors over the last few days, and I couldn't afford to forget that.

Still, my thought earlier remained true: there was something strange about Elias.

# CHAPTER THIRTEEN

I couldn't find the shirt I was supposed to be wearing for my meeting with a venue that morning.

It wasn't a huge deal, as I'd just replenished my dwindling supply of clean laundry the night before, but still, it didn't make sense that of the three shirts I had left hanging in my closet the night before, my favorite was missing. I knew I hadn't worn it, so what could've happened to it?

I cursed under my breath as I glanced at the clock with no time to worry about it. I needed to get on the road before traffic made me late. Living so close to work had done little for my timekeeping, as I never seemed to give myself enough wiggle room anymore.

I pulled on a different shirt, buttoning it up carefully and wrapping a tie around my neck. I tied it as I tried to kick my shoes in place, bending down to slip my feet inside them once the tie was straightened.

I threw on my jacket next and rushed from my room,

thankful Elias was nowhere to be seen. I couldn't deal with him that morning. I didn't even have time to make myself breakfast. I needed to leave—I glanced at my phone—ten minutes ago. I grabbed my keys from the counter and shoved my phone into my pocket, pulling open the door and rushing down the hall as quickly as I could. As I neared the parking garage, I felt my phone vibrating in my pocket, and I hurriedly dug it back out.

*Addy.*

"Good morning," I sang into the phone.

"Did you tell your daughter she could go to Venice before we came to an official decision?" She was angry, her voice agitated and shrill. We'd been in such a good place last night.

"Um, no, of course I didn't. Why?"

"Well, she says you did. I know I said I wanted her to get as much experience as she could, but I didn't say for sure that I wanted her to go."

"What are you talking about? I didn't tell her yes, Addy, I swear. I told her I'd have to talk to you, just like I told you last night. I haven't talked to her since then. If she told you I said yes last night, she's just lying to try to get you to say yes."

"No, Wes. You're lying. She showed me your text. *I'll talk to your mom. Just give me some time. I see Venice in your future, kiddo.* Really, Wes? Make me out to be the bad guy when I was the one leaning toward yes last night?"

"I honestly have no idea what you're talking about." I stopped walking, staring around the garage as I searched for my car. Where had I left it? "I didn't tell her yes. I didn't text her. Are you sure she isn't just teasing you? Maybe she faked the message with an app or something."

"Why would she do that?"

I spun around, my heart thudding in my chest. Where was my car? I'd been so distracted the night before I hadn't paid attention to where I'd parked. Finally, out of the corner of my eye I spied the silver BMW and rushed toward it.

"Why would she do that, Wes?" she repeated.

"Oh, um, I don't know. Because she's mad at me? Because she wants us to give in? Name a reason, and I'm sure you'd be right." I pressed the button on my fob and settled into the car, buckling up as it connected to Bluetooth before I whipped out of the parking spot.

"You really think I'm stupid, don't you?" she spat. "I wanted to believe you'd changed, Wes." She laughed under her breath sarcastically. "I thought after last night…" I heard the exasperated breath through the line.

"Wait, hold on, I *have* changed, Addy. I'm doing everything I can to prove that to you. What else could you possibly want from me?"

"I want you to be honest with me—"

"I am being honest with you! I don't know anything about a text message. I didn't tell Rory she could go to Venice. Frankly, I don't want her to go at all, but I'm going to respect whatever choice you make. I have no idea why she's lying to you, but I didn't do this."

"I'm staring at the text message, Wes. A message that clearly came from your phone."

"Look," I glanced at the clock as I pulled out of the

garage and into traffic, "there has to be some kind of mix-up. I honestly have no idea what you're talking about, but I know I didn't send any kind of text. I'm driving right now, so I can't check my phone, but once I get to work, I'll look at it and see if I can figure out what's going on. Whatever it is, though, I'm telling you I didn't send the message. If you want me to tell Rory that, I will. Trust me, I'd be more than happy to. I don't want her to go to Italy. I told you the same thing last night. More than that, I don't want to fight with you, babe. I am changing, and last night was great. It felt like we were getting back to our old selves. Please don't let this ruin that."

"That's just it, Wes. That's what I've been telling you, and you just don't seem to get it. I don't want to get back to our old selves. Our old selves haven't worked for me for a long time. You know that."

I crossed over into the next lane, and someone behind me laid on their horn. I looked into the rearview mirror, spotting the black, jacked-up truck and its oversized, angry driver. "That's not what I meant. A better version of our old selves, you know? The people we were when things were good."

"I'm just not sure there's any part of them left. Last night was wishful thinking. I wanted to believe we could fix this, Wes, but we can't. This…this whole situation is a startling reminder of that."

"I don't understand why this is such a big deal. I'm telling you I didn't send the message. I'll deal with Rory. I'll deal with everything. What else do you want me to do, Addy?"

"I want you to stop lying to me!" she cried. "I've spent so long being lied to by you about your late nights and broken promises. There's always an excuse with you. You were stuck in traffic, you had a last minute change of venue, your client had a meltdown, your *boss* had a meltdown. Always, always an excuse, and...what is it this time? You expect me to believe your phone got hacked?"

*Hacked...*

Her words reminded me of the situation at work. Was it possible this was somehow related? "Actually, I'm not being facetious, but we just had a hack at work. I access my work email on my phone. It's possible I was hacked. *Shit.* I didn't even think of that." My breathing quickened. "I'll have to check and see—"

She scoffed, interrupting me. "Are you serious right now? Do you truly expect me to believe that you were hacked and someone sent a text message through your phone just to screw with us?"

"I'm being serious. It's true. I'm not lying to you right now. We really were hacked. I don't know that it's related, but I don't know that it wasn't—"

"How would anyone else even know about Italy? Did you tell anyone?"

"No, of course not."

"Well, then how would they know?"

"I agree, it doesn't make sense. That's why I think it had to be Rory."

She groaned. "Ugh, Wes, I can't deal with this right now. I've got to get to work."

"No, wait, Addy, please!" But it was no use. The line

was dead and she was gone, and just like that, every bit of happiness I'd had the night before was gone with her.

---

WHEN I ARRIVED at the office, I checked my phone straight away, anxious to make sure I hadn't somehow texted her in my sleep, but just as I'd suspected, there was nothing to confirm any of what Addy had said.

Rory had to have crafted the text message herself somehow, but I wanted to check everything out to be sure.

Instead of going to my office, I headed to the back, past the break room and knocked on Oliver's door.

"Come in," he said, and I pushed the door open. "Hey, Wes, what's up?"

"Hey, I wanted to check with you about something."

"Sure," Oliver said, turning away from his computer. He folded his hands in front of him, watching me carefully.

"After the hack, Stewart said we should change our passwords on our phones too, just in case they'd gained access to something there through our email or the client portal. So, I did. I changed everything, even Facebook and Instagram, just to be on the safe side."

"Sure, sure..."

"But this morning my wife said I'd texted my daughter something that I know I didn't."

"Okay..." he said, looking up toward his eyebrows in thought.

"So, I guess what I'm asking is, could they have somehow gained access to my text messages?"

"Well, I guess it's possible," he said, drawing out the word. "But all signs point to no. We haven't found any proof that the hacker gained access to anything. Phones aren't easy to access, especially, what is it you have there, an iPhone…" He clicked his tongue. "Yeah, that would be a doozy. I'll tell you what, though, if it'll make you feel better, I can run a few scans on it, do a few tests, and make sure everything looks good."

"Could you?" I asked. "That would be amazing."

"Yeah, sure thing. Do you want to leave it with me for an hour or two? I can bring it to you when I'm done." He held out his hand, and I laid the phone in it.

"Thanks so much, Oliver. I owe you."

"Consider us even after the other day, man, okay? It's not a problem at all."

I patted the desk and departed his office, heading back to my own.

Like he'd promised, a few hours later, Oliver returned with my phone. He waved it in the air. "Good news, bad news."

"Okay." I braced myself for the worst.

"Good news, I ran three different antivirus systems through your phone and didn't find anything out of the ordinary. So, it's clean. You're good there. Bad news is that it still doesn't explain your text message dilemma. Now, I've heard of this happening before, it's rare, but not rare enough, where people have had their phones cloned."

"Cloned?"

"Hackers basically make a copy of the phone, and they

can control it remotely. Like I said, it's way less common than a virus, but it would explain a text message being sent from your line if you're sure you didn't do it."

"Okay," I said, trying not to panic. "So, what does that mean? What do I do?"

"Well, you've already done some of what I'd suggest right away, making sure you changed all your passwords. Does that include your banking, your emails…"

I nodded along. "Yes. Yes."

"Okay, good. That's the biggest thing. Have you noticed your phone overheating any? Or when you're on calls, do you ever hear clicking noises in the background?"

"No," I said. "Nothing like that."

"Those are big signs, so you should be on the lookout. That's a dramatic conclusion, but I did want to make you aware. You should keep an eye on your phone bill, too. If you see any calls or texts that you didn't send, you need to get a new phone straight away, 'cause you've definitely been cloned."

"But wouldn't the antivirus get rid of the clone?"

"Sometimes," he said, "but not always. You could try factory resetting your phone too, if you're worried about it. But…" I could tell he was registering the stress on my expression. "I mean, if it's just a one-off with a text message, who knows. I just wanted to warn you, just in case. I'm sure there's some other explanation."

I nodded, staring at the phone. Suddenly, Elias' sticky note over the webcam didn't seem so crazy. "Well, I appreciate you checking it out for me. I'll keep a close eye on things."

"Sure thing," he said, reopening the door. "Holler if

you need me for anything else or if it starts acting up again, but short of factory resetting it, the next best thing if it does is to get a new device entirely." He paused. "Let's hope it doesn't come to that."

"Yep, definitely. I'm sure it was just a miscommunication. I appreciate it." When he left my office, I tucked my phone in my drawer for safekeeping…just in case.

## CHAPTER FOURTEEN

I was distracted by the argument all day, hardly able to focus as I toured a new venue and negotiated contracts for two of my clients. The deals were good, but even as I delivered the news, I couldn't bring myself to celebrate.

I bounced back and forth between worry over my phone and frustration about how I'd ever get Addy to believe that I hadn't sent the message. The easiest explanation was that Rory had crafted the message, but I had no idea why my daughter was working to tear us apart if that were the case. Perhaps it was simple shortsightedness and she'd believed lying was the easiest path to getting her way.

I thought briefly of asking Elias what he could tell me about apps that could create fake text messages or the idea that someone may have hacked or cloned my phone somehow, but decided against it. As much as I wanted to, I still couldn't bring myself to trust him completely. And besides, like Addy had pointed out, no one else knew about Italy. It had to be Rory. It was the only explanation.

Still, I'd changed my passwords on my phone yet again, feeling uneasy about everything that had happened and having no idea where to direct the emotion.

After a long day of zoning out, having to ask people to repeat themselves, and having to reread entire paragraphs of contracts, when I looked up and realized it was after four o'clock and I still needed to get across town to pick up Rory, my heart fell.

I'd been so distracted, I hadn't even noticed time creeping by as quickly as it did.

I stood from my desk, logging off the computer and rushing out of the office and straight to my car. I connected my Bluetooth and instructed it to call Addy. It was my third time calling her since our hang up, so I didn't expect her to answer this time either, but I had to try.

After one ring, it went to her voicemail. "Hey, I'm on my way to pick up Rory for soccer... I'm, uh, I'm hoping to see you so we can talk about things. We probably won't have time before, but I'm going to talk to her on the way there, and maybe we can all sit down and talk when she's done." I paused, not sure what else to say. "Anyway, I'll see you in a bit. Call me back if you can. I...I love you." I felt the need to apologize, though I had nothing to apologize for, so I chose to end the call instead.

I bobbed and weaved through traffic, catching a few middle fingers and horns, but I honestly didn't care. I needed to get to Rory as quickly as possible. If I was late again, especially with Addy already mad at me, there was a good chance she'd void our agreement entirely.

As I veered off onto the exit that would take me onto the interstate, my phone began ringing, the shrill sound of my Bluetooth's ringer carrying through the car. I hit the button on my steering wheel to answer the call.

At least she was calling me back now. "Hey!"

"Hey, Wes." She sounded exhausted. As if she was dreading talking to me. Maybe I'd become exhausting.

"Listen, I just want to say—"

"You don't have to come pick Rory up," she said at the same time.

"Wait, what?" I demanded. "Now that's not fair. I know you're mad, but you can't punish me like this. We agreed I'd take her to practice on Thursdays. That was the deal."

"I know what the deal was, but she got a ride from one of her friends."

"How could you let that happen? You knew I was coming to get her."

"Truth be told, it slipped my mind. Today's been nothing but an argument with her. She's furious because she feels like you told her she could go and now we're ripping that away from her, and... She just needs some space. She deserves some space to work through it. She's just a kid, Wes, and we're putting her through a lot."

"I know she's just a kid," I said angrily. I wanted to argue about the text message, but, at the same time, I just wanted to bring peace to the situation. "I just hate it. We didn't get much time together last night, and I was really looking forward to tonight."

"Trust me, you would've spent the whole time arguing with her tonight anyway. Just give her the week, okay? Check back in next week once she's had some time to cool off."

I groaned internally but kept it hidden from my voice. "Fine. That's fine. Who did she go with?"

"The boy I told you she's been talking to. His name's Brody."

The hairs on my arms stood up. "Brody? Who the hell is Brody?"

"He goes to school in Smyrna. They met on an app."

"On an app? How old is he? Do we know him?"

She sighed. "Don't freak out over this. He's just taking her to practice, okay? I've got her location on my phone. It's fine. She's getting old enough to start dating."

"Sixteen. We agreed she could date at sixteen. We've still got two years."

"Yes, well, I guess we never discussed the appropriate age for her to get a ride from a friend."

"Is he her friend or is he a *boy*friend?"

"A little of both, maybe. Listen, I don't want you to worry about this or lecture her. She's really excited about this one. God knows she needs something to be excited about these days. And we need something to earn us brownie points. I've already told her we're going to have to have dinner together and meet him soon, but I didn't see the harm in him driving her to practice and bringing her back home after. If anything, it's a nice gesture that he's supporting her."

"We'll have to meet him soon? You didn't meet him when he picked her up?"

"No. She asked me if he could pick her up from school, and I said yes."

"Jesus Christ, this kid could be a serial killer."

"He's not a serial killer," she said with a dry laugh. "He's just a boy. A boy who your daughter really likes."

I shook my head, turning my blinker on and veering into the right lane to take the next exit. "Well, I don't like it, for the record. She's not old enough for a boyfriend."

She laughed. "She is too. We started dating at sixteen, and you and I both had serious relationships before then. We'd be the biggest hypocrites in the world to make a big deal about this. We can't keep her locked away forever."

The thought made me sick. The very idea of her dating was bad enough, but for her to date when I wasn't there to meet her date at the door was maddening. I wanted to look him in the eye, get to know him a bit before I let him drive off with my little girl.

"Well, if she's gone and apparently I get no say in the matter, do you think I could come over so we can talk? I hate the way we left things this morning. I've been thinking about it all day."

She hesitated, and I felt a sinking feeling in my stomach, bracing me for the fall.

"I just don't think it's a good idea right now."

"Last night was so—"

"Good, yeah, I know. It was. And I got caught up in it. You're very good at making me forget why we're doing this in the first place. We have to keep to the agreement. You can help out, spend time with Rory, but we're on the brink of divorce, Wes. I can't let you make me forget that just by flashing your schoolboy grin at me."

I hadn't heard the last half of her statement because it was the first time I'd heard her say the word *divorce* so plainly. I felt my insides clench, her words echoing in my ears. "We're on the brink of divorce?"

She hesitated, and I realized she hadn't meant to say it. At least, not aloud. "I scheduled a meeting with a lawyer this morning," she said softly. I could practically see her wincing as she said the words. "I was going to tell you—"

"When? When were you going to tell me? This seems completely out of nowhere."

"Does it, though? You've moved out, Wes. I've asked you to get your own place. We're working through custody."

"But you never said you were actually considering divorcing me. I've even asked you, and you've never said it like that. I thought you just needed some space for a bit."

"I do. But space has been nice. It's shown me where we were lacking. And it's made me doubt whether or not we can fix it." She paused. "Rory told me you were late last night. On the first night, Wes. It's just so reminiscent of every night for the past few years. Ever since we moved to Green Hills, ever since you took this job, you've just been different. And I'm happy for you. I'm so happy for you. I know you love your job, and I know you're so happy—"

"I'm not happy without you. Is it about my job? I've told you I'll quit, Addy. I'll quit tomorrow. We'll move. We'll start over. We'll be better. This isn't what I want. I don't want to lose you."

"It's not the job. It's not the house. It's you, Wes." She was crying then. "I don't want you to have to leave a job you love; I just want you to do better. If you're late when you're trying to prove yourself, why would I ever believe things would change when you're back home and things are normal again?"

"I had a long day at work, and traffic was a mess—"

"Yeah," she said quickly, sniffling. "There's always an excuse. That's what I've learned. Always. And I'm not saying you're lying, but this isn't working for me. Having a husband who can't seem to fit his family into his schedule isn't working for me. I got caught up in the moment last night, Wes. I did. Because you're charming and you remind me of what used to be and... I still love you. Of course I do. But that doesn't matter anymore. I shouldn't have let you stay later last night. That wasn't fair to either of us. I wish things could be different. It would be easier if I could just pretend everything was fixed. God, it would be so much easier. But I can't. I just need time. You can still come over on Wednesdays, but it's so you can spend time with Rory. Not me. We both have to remember that. You should get yourself a lawyer, too. I want to keep things civil and fair."

"I don't want a lawyer. I don't want any of this. Can we just—"

"I'm sorry, I have to go. I have to take this call. We'll talk soon."

With that, she ended the call. There was no goodbye, just the sudden absence of her voice in the car. Just like the absence of her in my life. I had no idea what had gone wrong, what had changed so much since the night before.

Besides the text message. That was what it all came down to, but the text was obviously just Rory's way of acting out because she wasn't getting her way. It had to be. Nothing else made sense.

Why was my daughter determined to ruin things for me?

Why was Addy so willing to let her?

I was doing my best to fix everything between the three of us. Why wasn't that good enough?

# CHAPTER FIFTEEN

Fifteen minutes later, I pulled back into the parking garage. I felt strangely numb. I hadn't felt this way since I was in high school, getting my heart broken by girls whose names I couldn't even remember now. When I looked at my past, all I saw was Addy.

But Addy had never hurt me like this.

She'd never given up on me.

Was I going to end up divorced? Truly? I couldn't believe I wasn't going to be able to get myself out of the mess somehow. There was always a way. I'd moved in with Elias in order to make Addy happy, but I didn't want to stay there long term. I wanted to go home. I wanted to fix this, I just didn't know how.

If we were truly going to get divorced, I needed to get my own place. I needed to get a second job to afford a second place. We needed to list the house and start dividing our limited assets. We'd have to decide on a custody arrangement.

I couldn't even bear to think about all it would entail as I made my way up the stairs and to the apartment.

Once inside, I saw Elias on the couch, his legs curled up under him as he scribbled through an oversized book of Sudoku puzzles.

"Hey," he said, looking up with a confused look on his face as I shut the door. "What's the matter? I thought you weren't going to be home tonight."

"Yeah, I had a change of plans," I said with all the positivity I could muster, which wasn't a lot.

"What happened?"

I couldn't hold it in. I sank into the couch, shaking my head as I stared into space. "I think I'm getting divorced." I didn't want to talk about it, but I desperately needed someone to make it make sense for me.

He slammed the book shut, setting it on the couch next to him, pencil on top. "I'm sorry, man. I thought you guys were working things out."

"I thought so, too," I said, gathering my hands in my lap and staring down at them, focusing on not letting the tears I felt brimming, fall. "She's already talking to an attorney. I don't know if there's anything I can do to fix this. I think…" I looked up at him, meeting his eye. "I think she's made up her mind."

Sorrow filled his expression, and he cocked his head to the side. As much as Elias may annoy me, I honestly wouldn't have wanted to have this discussion with anyone else. It was true what he'd said that first night at the bar. Toxic masculinity didn't seem to exist with him. Emotions were not only allowed, but encouraged. Talking seemed to be the highlight of his afternoon. It was so different than any friendship I'd ever experienced.

"I'm so sorry, Wes. Maybe she just needs a little space. I'm sure she'll come around."

"I don't think so," I said. "I've tried. I tried doing all she wanted. I tried talking things out. I did everything... She didn't even tell me until she'd already hired an attorney. I'm not honestly sure where she got the money to do it. Probably Vivi."

"Vivi?" he asked, his thick brows knitting together.

"Her mom."

He nodded, seeming to understand. "Well, if you need the money to hire an attorney yourself, I'm happy to let you borrow some."

"No," I said quickly, though I realized a second later that I may actually have to take him up on that. "She said I should, but I'm not ready to do that."

"Well, the offer stands," he said simply. "I'm sorry. I know how much she means to you."

"She means everything," I said, and I felt the first tear begin to fall. I kept my chin tucked to my chest, refusing to acknowledge that it was happening or wipe the tear away. I needed to get to my bedroom, but I couldn't move.

"Life sucks sometimes," he said sadly. "It really, really does. I wish there was something I could do. Maybe she just needs a bit of time to realize how much she misses you."

I sniffled. "Maybe."

"You two belong together. You'll see, she'll come around."

"I offered to quit my job for her," I said. "That job means everything to me. I've worked so hard to get it, and I would throw it away tomorrow if it meant getting her back."

"You shouldn't have to do that. You shouldn't be the one sacrificing everything."

"It doesn't matter. Even that wasn't enough. She's over me. She all but said that."

Elias hung his head. "I'm really sorry, Wes."

"Thanks." I sniffled loudly, running the back of my hand under my nose. "I'm sorry to be dragging you in the middle of everything. You don't need this right now."

"Hey, don't worry about that," he said, resting a hand on my arm for a second before pulling it away. "That's what friends are for. I'm happy to help you work through all of this. I've had my heart broken before, and I was a much bigger mess than you are right now. I thought I'd never get over it. I totally get how you're feeling. Probably better than most people."

"Really?" It was hard for me to picture Elias heartbroken.

"I'm thirty-two and single. You think I haven't had my share of heartbreak?"

I couldn't help smiling as he read my mind. "I guess that's true."

"Yeah. And hey, you know what helped in the end? Moving on to other things I enjoyed. Video games, Sudoku, a weekend away at a Comic-Con. What do you enjoy doing?"

I thought for a moment, unable to answer the question. "I have no idea." I hadn't been able to spend a day doing anything I enjoyed in years. I'd forgotten what hobbies were.

"Well, why don't we invite a few people over. We can have a bit of fun and get your mind off everything for the night. Everybody relaxes after a few drinks. You've been working so hard. You deserve a night to decompress. Seriously, between work and doing everything Addy asks of you, you hardly eat, hardly sleep. You're working your-self to the bone to fix things, and if she can't see what a great guy you are, it's her loss."

I looked up then, aware of the tears on my cheeks. Elias didn't acknowledge them. He just waited for me to respond. "Thanks," I said finally. "I'm just not sure I'm up to doing anything tonight. I should probably catch up on work."

He twisted his mouth, obviously wanting to say something.

"I know, I shouldn't be working."

"It's not that. I mean, no, you shouldn't, but...I should've told you, but I didn't think it would matter. I kind of already invited people over when I thought you weren't going to be home tonight. A few friends." He paused. "I can cancel if you're not up to it."

"No. No, of course not. Don't be silly. I'll probably just try and catch up on some sleep anyway. Don't cancel on my account."

"I really couldn't relax with my friends knowing you were having such a lousy night in your room alone. Won't you just try and have fun tonight? I think you could really use it. And, don't worry. It's just a few of the people I game with. We'll be drinking a few beers and playing all night. Nothing too wild."

I thought for a moment. Elias was probably the only person on my side of things in the world, so I didn't want to squander his loyalty. "Okay, yeah. I can always use a beer."

"Attaboy," he said, patting my shoulder. "If there's anything I'm an expert at, it's being heartbroken. You couldn't have asked for someone more experienced to help you get through this. And you will. You'll get through it."

I offered him a small, appreciative smile. Strange as he was, Elias was just what I needed; he was right about that. As he sank back onto the couch and flipped on the TV, he smiled at me encouragingly, and I promised myself I would do whatever I could to play the part that night.

I needed to have fun for Elias.

Soon, he might be all I had left.

# CHAPTER SIXTEEN

E lias' friends showed up at half past six, and they were nothing like I'd expected.

He'd invited four of them. Stephanie had pixie-cut black hair and wore combat boots as well as an oversized, olive green military-style jacket. She had a piercing in the center space between her upper lip and nose and wore thick eyeliner and dark, purple lipstick.

Ariel was less eccentric, with light brown hair that rested just above her shoulders, a hoodie, Converse, and no makeup. She smelled of fried food.

Mac, on the other hand, smelled like cigarettes. He was wafer-thin, like Elias, and had shaggy blond hair and an eyebrow piercing.

Garth was soft spoken, while the others were loud, and he wore his hair neatly trimmed, though his Nirvana T-shirt and skinny jeans were stained up, and I was pretty sure he was high on something other than life.

All in all, they were nothing like Elias, and from all I knew about him, and how often he'd told me he didn't really have friends, they all seemed to know each other quite well. They crammed onto the two small couches in the living room, leaving me with the executive, rolling computer chair Elias had pulled from his bedroom.

They seemed fascinated by me, asking questions about my work and my marriage without regard for privacy or civility. At least they seemed to share that trait with their friend.

A few beers in, and everyone, myself included, had seemed to loosen up quite a bit. At some point, Stephanie came over and sat on the ground near my legs as we watched Garth and Elias facing off in some sort of combat round on the video game.

Mac lit up a cigarette, not bothering to ask if it would bother anyone, and blew his smoke into the room. It took me back to my college days: a smoky room, drinks spread out across the table, and bodies everywhere.

Stephanie reached over, playing with the hem of my pants. "So, what sort of things does a booking agent do, exactly?" she asked, having to shout over the game.

I leaned down closer to her, solely so we could hear each other better, and said, "Mostly book venues for my clients, find them gigs, and schedule appearances. Occasionally, I'll sign us new clients, if I'm downtown and overhear someone I think is talented, but that's rare."

"It sounds so exciting. So you actually get to work with celebrities?"

One side of my mouth lifted into an easy smile. "Yeah."

"What is that like? I'd be such a nervous wreck."

I focused on her lip ring, watching the silver ball bounce as she talked. For some reason, I couldn't picture

Stephanie getting nervous about anything. Everything about her was bold and confident, including her hand on my calf. "Nah, you get used to it. It's pretty cool when you get backstage access to some of the bigger shows, but at the end of the day, it's just a job."

"You must love it, though," she said, and I felt the bitterness rising in my chest again. Truth was, I wasn't sure I'd loved it in a very long time, but no one had bothered to ask until Elias had that night at the bar. It was the first time I'd allowed myself to really process my feelings for my career in so long. Of course, her quasi-question didn't require that detailed of a response.

Instead, I went with, "Parts of it, yeah."

"Who's the biggest celebrity you've ever met?" Ariel asked from across the room.

I cleared my throat and took another drink of my beer. It was room temperature by that point. "Um, well, that's hard to say. I've met most of the stars here, honestly. I did get to meet Dolly Parton, though. It was kind of by accident, but she's one of the sweetest people I've ever met. Obviously not my client, but such a cool experience. That's probably my favorite celebrity experience."

"No kidding?" Stephanie's eyes widened. "I'm *obsessed* with her. I grew up listening to her music. She has the best story ever."

"Yeah, she's super cool," Ariel agreed.

"You got a picture with her, didn't you?" Elias asked. "On your desk. I think I remember seeing it." I hadn't even known he'd been listening, and he wasn't looking our way, making me question whether he was even talking to me at first.

"Yeah, I do," I said, nodding slowly.

"*No way*. Ugh, I'm so jealous," Stephanie said.

"That's amazing," Ariel agreed.

"My brother's a bouncer. He's met some cool people, too," Mac added, though no one seemed to pay him any attention.

"You should see the pictures he has in his office. He's met everyone," Elias said.

"Can we see?" Stephanie begged, her hands held in front of her as if she were praying. "Please. I'm totally celeb-obsessed. I read gossip magazines like they're my Bible."

"Oh, I don't know... We're not really supposed to have people in the office unless they're clients."

"Oh, come on, please? I swear I won't touch anything. They'll never even know I was there. You'd be my favorite person in the world." She put her hands on my knees, and though I doubted there was any ulterior motive, my skin was suddenly on fire, and I could focus on nothing else.

"Is your office on Music Row?" Ariel asked.

"Mhm," I said, my eyes still on Stephanie as she pushed her bottom lip out further in a pout.

"That is so cool. My bank works with so many celebrities, and they have all this signed stuff at the Music Row branch. Even a Hank Williams outfit that he actually wore. It's out of my way, but I go there every chance I get. It's...amazing." She closed her eyes, taking in a deep breath. "If I ever got to meet a celebrity, I'd probably die then and there."

"And if it was T-Swift, forget about it," Ariel added with a laugh.

Stephanie's eyes bulged. "Abso-freakin-lutely. I'm a total Swiftie. She's perfection." She looked back at me. "Have you ever met her?"

"Years ago, yeah. I wasn't even an agent then, though, just an intern. I probably have a picture somewhere."

She squealed. "Was she amazing? I'll bet she was amazing."

"Amazing," I confirmed.

"Are you sure you can't take us to see your collection? Oh, it would just make my night."

I sighed. It was incredibly tempting as she leaned closer to me, her entire body pressed to my calf, but I knew Stewart would have a fit.

"I'm sorry. I really wish I could—"

"Wes isn't the boss, Stephanie," Elias said, coming to my rescue. "He's probably not allowed to go into the office after hours anyway. You're barking up the wrong tree."

She let go of my leg, sinking back away from me with drooping shoulders. "Oh." She was visibly disappointed, and I felt the energy in the room shift.

Technically, I *was* allowed to go into the office whenever I wanted, I just wasn't allowed to bring anyone with me. I toyed with the idea. It wasn't like anyone had to know. I could say I'd needed to get my laptop. We could go in, look at the pictures, not disturb anything, and get out.

"Do you have any pictures on your phone?" Mac asked, almost as a challenge.

"I do, actually." I pulled out my phone, searching back through an album to find the photos from the festival last summer. I held my phone out to Stephanie once I'd landed on the ones I was searching for. "Here you go."

Stephanie took the phone from my hand, scrolling through the photos, her squeals growing louder with each new celebrity. "You are officially the coolest person I know!" she announced, standing up and throwing herself onto my lap before wrapping her arms around my neck. The chair rolled backward with the sudden shift in weight, and she squealed with delight. "You have to tell me everything. What are they like? Are they jerks? Who's the nicest? Who's the meanest?" I couldn't focus on anything but her body pressed against mine, her arm around my neck, a finger tracing a line across the collar of my shirt.

Garth grinned slyly at me, but I hardly noticed. I should've told her to get off. I should've mentioned that I was still married, despite telling them just moments ago that I was sure my wife was leaving me, but I couldn't.

I couldn't deny how good the attention felt and how badly I needed something, anything, to feel good.

"I can tell you anything you want to know. Most of these were just photos backstage, but some of them I know really well. Most of them are cool dudes. Kane is one of the most down-to-earth guys you'll ever meet, and Luke is hilarious." She nestled in closer to me as I scrolled through the pictures with her, telling her about each pictured celebrity.

"Do you ever get to bring guests to these events? There's not much I wouldn't do to meet any of these people," she said when I'd run out of stories to tell several minutes later.

"And she means *not much*," Mac said with an irritated groan.

"Ease up, Mac," Elias said. "Let her fangirl for a bit."

At his word, Mac grew quiet. I hadn't realized Elias was the unofficial leader of the group, but I noticed it then, the way they all responded to his words.

Stephanie rested her head on my shoulder. "He's not wrong," she said with a dry laugh. "I told you I'm a sucker for celebrity gossip. It's one of the reasons I'm planning to move to LA next year."

In unison, the group groaned.

"What? I am!" she said adamantly, sitting up to argue with them.

"Yeah, we know. You've been planning to move to LA next year for the last six years," Ariel said, downing the last of her beer and standing up, heading for the kitchen.

"Yeah, well, this is my year. I can feel it in my bones."

"That's just Wes you're feeling," Mac said, his joke met with uproarious laughter from all around. I adjusted uncomfortably, but Stephanie leaned back down, her lips on my ear.

"Don't let him bother you. Mac's just Mac."

"You can stop acting like a groupie, Steph. It's not like he's going to give you a lock of hair. If he could introduce you to anyone, he would've offered," Elias said with a laugh. "I told you, he's not the boss. He can't do stuff like that."

His words rubbed me the wrong way, and I felt my body stiffen. "I definitely don't have locks of hair, but actually, there is something I can get for you."

The room grew quiet, and Stephanie looked back at

me as if I were the tree on Christmas morning. "What's that?"

"I have a box of signed CDs left over from promotions we've done in the past. I could get you a few of the best ones, if you'd like that—"

She launched forward, pressing her lips to mine briefly and without warning. When we separated, she stood up, holding out her hand to me. "Come on! Come on now. You are amazing, Wes. You've made my day. What are you waiting for? Oh, I'll owe you so big. Who do you have? Can I have one of everything? Oh my God, you are amazing!"

I couldn't stop the joy that filled me at making her so happy. When was the last time Addy had looked at me that way? I forced the thought of her out of my head. "I can't get them tonight, but I'll get them for you tomorrow and have Elias get them to you."

"No! Please. You can't make me wait. I won't survive it." She jumped up and down, her hands clasped in front of her chest. "Let's go now. Please. Please. Please. Please. Please."

I sighed, trying to work it out in my head. "Okay, well, maybe we can, but you'll have to wait outside. I can't bring you in the building."

"Deal. Done. Whatever you need. Let's just go."

"I'll have to call an Uber," I said, wiggling the beer in my hand. "I'm probably okay to drive, but I just don't want to chance it."

"Mac can take us!" she cried, pointing to where he sat. He lifted his brow to look at her, apparently not all that enthused by the idea. "He doesn't drink, and he has a van. You can take us, can't you, Mac?"

"What do I get out of the deal?" he asked, licking his lips and adjusting the knees of his pants with a smirk.

"Maybe Wes can get you an autograph, too?" she asked, nodding her head at me.

Before I could respond, Mac scoffed. "I don't want a signature from some random person I've never met. Celebrity or not, that stuff just doesn't faze me. I've told you...I don't get the fascination."

"Well, fine, you'll get the joy of making your good friend super happy, then."

"Nah, I need gas money and a blowie."

She groaned. "In your dreams. I'd sooner blow a beer bottle."

Mac leaned forward, grabbing a chip from the open bag on the table. "Dinner and a show. Sounds like my kinda night."

She rolled her eyes, but I could tell she was enjoying the attention. Her cheeks were pink, either from the alcohol or excitement. Maybe both. "So will you take us or not?"

"You know I will," he said finally, standing up and running his hands down his legs. Elias paused the game, looking around.

"All right," he said, apparently on board with the plan. "What do you say, guys? Road trip?"

"Road trip!" Stephanie called, one fist in the air dramatically as she let out a whoop.

The rest of the group echoed the cry as if we were

headed on a spring break trip rather than just across town, and Elias turned off the TV.

Just like that, we were on our way to the door and Stephanie grabbed my hand, lacing her fingers through mine.

It was a mistake. The entire night. I knew it before we'd taken a step out the door, but I didn't pull away.

Not then and not as we all piled into Mac's rusted blue minivan that reeked of cigarette smoke and dirty socks. Elias took the front seat, Ariel and Garth were in the middle, and Stephanie pulled me to the back.

I'd never cheated on my wife, for the record. My only mistress was my job. I loved Addy and she was truly the only woman I wanted in my life, but I couldn't deny the way Stephanie's affection made my sadness less noticeable, the way it seemed to dull the heartache.

If Addy wanted a divorce, I needed to find a way to cope, and this wasn't the worst idea I could think of.

She kept her hand locked with mine, her head on my shoulder as I directed Mac toward my office building and then into the empty parking garage. They all cheered when my pass got us through the gates without having to pay, and I felt my adrenaline buzzing.

It was as if I were back in high school, high off the attention that being popular had brought me.

I was a broke kid with parents who were too busy to pay me any attention, but the kids at school didn't seem to notice. I was good-looking and smart—even at an early age—witty and clever, and always athletic. The attention and popularity were the only reasons I made it through school; they'd kept me afloat, giving me reasons to keep returning.

I felt the same way then. Even Mac, as much as he couldn't stand me, seemed to turn his attention to me when he thought I wouldn't notice. I was used to the jealousy, too. It was why I'd been so happy to reconnect with Elias. Anyone who could remember me from back then—who could see that I was able to find a way to be just as high up and enviable now as I had been back then, even at the lowest point in my life with my impending divorce—only served to inflate my ego.

I hated myself for crying in front of him earlier. How had I let myself be so vulnerable? I couldn't do that anymore.

It was why I leaned into Stephanie's advances even more, using my thumb to caress her hand as it gripped mine.

Once we were parked, I made a move to climb out of the van. "Okay, I'll be right back," I called as I jumped down, but Stephanie was coming out behind me. To my surprise, they were all unbuckling. And, before I realized what was happening, the car doors were shut and all five of them were standing in front of me, waiting for me to lead the way.

Elias nodded encouragingly. "It's fine, Wes. They won't bother anything. Live a little, right?" His words left no room for negotiation and, at that point, I saw little use fighting it.

Even if I'd wanted to, Stephanie batted her eyes at me, her hands squeezed together in front of her chest once more. We were already there. Though I knew it was against the rules, we were already in the parking garage. I couldn't back out then.

"Okay," I said as I exhaled. "But no one can touch anything. We'll go straight to my office, get the CDs, and get out of there."

"Deal."

"Okay."

"Sounds good."

"You're the boss."

"Whatever you say."

The responses echoed through the quiet garage, and I turned, shoving down the sense of dread as I owned the role, feeling their excitement buzzing around me. I could live off of being able to impress others; it was how I'd managed to be promoted from Junior Agent to Agent so quickly. I'd spent my career always striving for the best deals, managing to score venues and artists that were considered impossible to get.

We quickly made our way through the parking garage, in the glass double doors, and inside the building. I shut off the alarm and led them through the open lobby, laden with intern desks, and to my office door. I turned the key and opened the door, letting them inside the usually airy office, though it was now crammed with all six of us inside. I watched Stephanie's eyes roam the shelves, her face filled with pure joy. She was notably the most enamored by it all, though they all seemed to be excited by my memorabilia, no matter how much Mac tried to hide it.

"This is the coolest collection I've ever seen," she said, nudging Ariel. "Look!" She pointed toward a picture of me backstage at the Opry standing next to a crowd of my clients, recognizable songwriters and a few performers. "I cannot believe you get to call this your job."

I smiled, pleased that I'd been able to live up to the hype. "I guess it is pretty unbelievable."

She ran her fingers across a golden frame, her lips pursed. "Elias, I can't believe you didn't tell us your room-mate was such a badass."

Elias chuckled. "Well sue me for keeping him to myself for a while."

"Well, no more of that now that Stephanie's dug her claws into him," Ariel said.

I let out a puff of breath, running my hands through my hair. Was that what she'd done? Did they think the two of us were going to be something? A shiver ran over my body. I was still a married man. I still loved my wife. Suddenly, I was overwhelmed with the urge to get out of the building. What was I thinking bringing them here? Reality smacked me in the face, the stupor of the evening disappearing in one quick wave.

I didn't even know these people. For all I knew, they were criminals.

I stepped forward, sticking my key into the desk to unlock it and open the bottom drawer. I dug through the CDs, grabbing one of each—twelve in total—and locking it back up. "Here you go," I told Stephanie. "I'm not sure which ones you want, but I can bring back any of them you don't want."

She held her hands out, gripping the CDs close to her chest. "No way. This is amazing. Thank you, thank you, thank you." She grinned gleefully, spinning around in a circle. "You have made my night, Wes."

"You're welcome," I said. "Some of them may be older. Like I said, they're all left over from promotions, ones that didn't get claimed."

She leaned forward, kissing my cheek briefly, and I was incredibly aware of everyone's eyes on us. "Okay, we should get going," I said, clearing my throat. My face burned with embarrassment as I wondered if they were going to argue. To my great relief, they filed out of my office without further coaxing and, once I'd locked the door behind me, Elias led the way toward the front of the lobby.

I set the alarm at the door and, together, we made it back out the two glass double doors. The second we stepped into the parking garage, I let out a sigh of relief. We'd made it. I'd done what we'd come to do—Stephanie had her autographs, everyone was relatively impressed with me, and nothing bad had happened. Stewart would never know.

I let out a heavy breath, the tension leaving my shoulders, and when the doors to the van opened, I made my way to the back to go through the CDs with Stephanie. I wanted to soak up any extra admiration I could from her.

I had a feeling I was going to be existing on that for quite a while, even if that was all I'd allow myself to receive from her.

When we made it back home, we settled into the living room once more. I took the chair again, and Stephanie asked me to recount stories about where the autographs had come from, wanting to know which celebrities used assistants to sign some of their autographs and which did it themselves every time.

I indulged her, and at the end of the night, when I led her to the door, drunk off her stares and the additional beers I'd had since we got back home, I still found the resolve to turn my head when she moved in for a kiss, letting it land on my cheek.

"I shouldn't," I told her softly, though I desperately wanted to. My head wasn't clear, but I knew I wouldn't forgive myself if I got carried away and did something I'd regret. If there was even a chance with Addy, I had to try. "I'm sorry."

Her expression said she'd been expecting it. "I get it. It's a shame, but I get it. I hope your wife realizes what she's missing, Wes. You're the real deal." She lifted a hand to my cheek, rubbing it cautiously before stepping back, gripping the plastic sack Elias had given her for her CDs, and waving over her shoulder.

"Bye, y'all. See you next time."

One by one, they filed out of the room until it was just Elias and me left.

When I turned around, he had a crooked grin on his face.

"What?" I asked, my face heating up. I rubbed the space on my cheek where her lips had been just moments earlier.

He sat back down, resting his head on the back of the couch. "I told you I knew how to heal a broken heart."

## CHAPTER SEVENTEEN

When I got home Friday night, Elias had promised a quiet, temptation-free evening of Netflix and beer. I found him sitting on the kitchen counter again, his legs curled up underneath him. This time, though, he was snacking on sour gummy worms, rather than Twizzlers.

When he saw me walk in the door, he slid off the counter and onto the floor, his face ashen. I wondered briefly if I'd caught him doing something embarrassing. "Hey," he said, shoving his hands into his pockets.

"Hey." I paused, laying my keys on the counter. "What's up?"

He ran a hand over the back of his neck. "I need to tell you something."

Panic washed over me. Those words had never brought me any sort of good news. "Okay… What is it?"

"You should probably sit."

I didn't dare move, the absolute worst possible scenarios running through my head. *Someone's dead. Someone's pregnant. Someone has cancer.*

"What is it, Elias? You're scaring me."

"It's about Addy…"

*Addy's dead. Addy's pregnant. Addy has cancer.*

"What about her?"

What had he done? Had he told her about last night? What did he know about Addy? Why would he know anything about my wife?

"I had a house call for a client in Green Hills today. One of my longtime clients. She lives over on Summer-wind Circle."

The name of my street had me holding my breath.

"Is that where you live? Where Addy lives? Or do you know someone who does?"

I nodded slowly. "We live there… How do you know that? Why are you asking?"

"I had no idea. I was just driving over, and I saw her walking out of the house. I caught a glimpse of her, and I thought she looked familiar, but it was a fast glimpse, so I could've been wrong."

"What's the big deal if you saw her?" My body hadn't let down its defenses yet. I knew something was coming. Something big.

"Well, the thing is…she wasn't alone."

"She was with Rory?" I knew that wasn't the case, but I had to ask. It couldn't be what I was thinking, what he was suggesting, and yet, I knew that's exactly what it was.

"She was with a man," he said sadly. "I wasn't sure whether to tell you."

"What kind of man?"

"I didn't get a good look. He had brown hair, maybe.

He was wearing a suit. He... She walked him to his car, and she kissed him."

The room grew smaller around me, my vision tunneling. No. It couldn't be true. I couldn't pretend I hadn't wondered, briefly, if an affair may have been the cause of Addy's sudden assertion that we should break up, but that didn't make it any easier to hear. It just couldn't be true.

"I'm sorry, man," he said, hanging his head. "I've debated back and forth all day about whether or not to tell you. It could've been someone else. They were at a two-story house with white brick. There were bushes in front of the windows and a two-car garage that was—"

"Detached," I finished for him. "I've gotta—" I didn't finish the sentence, but I don't think he expected me to. How could she do this to me? Why was she home in the middle of the day with some man? Who was he? I pulled my phone from my pocket, my jaw tight with sudden rage. I stormed past Elias, slamming the door. I could hear him still talking, apologizing, but I couldn't listen. I couldn't focus on anything else.

The line rang twice, and then I was sent to voicemail.

Without a second thought and completely blinded by my rage, I swung open the door again, rushed past Elias, and scooped up my keys from the counter.

"I'll be back," I called.

"Be careful. Do you want me to go—"

I'd already shut the door, interrupting his offer. There was no way I could allow Elias to come, because I was going to unleash the worst parts of myself on my wife. Angry, bitter tears filled my eyes as I barreled down the stairs and through the parking garage before climbing in the car and whipping out of the parking garage and away from downtown.

I tried to call her again on the way there, over and over again. Every time I'd hear the voicemail, I'd hang up and call again. She'd either answer or I'd get there first. Either way, she wasn't going to get away with her lie anymore. If she was going to leave me for someone else, there was no way she was going to keep up the charade that the fault lay with me. If she was woman enough to have an affair, she was going to be woman enough to look me in the eye and tell me about it herself.

As I arrived in Green Hills, I'd given up trying to call. I was only minutes from home and still trying to prepare myself for what I would say. Truth was, if she'd answered I was sure I would've rambled and cried, unable to form coherent thoughts. But now, I'd had enough practice, enough time to think. And still, I had nothing good to say.

How could you do this to me? I'd beg.

How could you let me fight so hard to fix things, blame myself for everything going wrong, hate myself for not doing everything I could to make things better when I'd had the chance. And all along, it had been her. Not me. I hadn't been the one that made the fatal mistake.

I may not be blameless, but the blame assigned to me was significantly less than I'd been made to believe.

I pulled into the driveway, noting that both doors to the garage were closed, which could mean that the strange man was still there, that my mother-in-law was there, or that no one was there at all. I'd be completely surprised, as would whoever was waiting on the other side of the door.

I practically launched myself from the car when it rolled to a stop, and I hurried up the walk quickly. When I reached the door, I rapped my knuckles against the wood, already digging in my pocket for my keys.

This was still my house, dammit, and there was no way in hell I was going to hand it over just because she'd fallen for someone else. Why should I have to uproot my life when it was she who had made the decision to end things?

Everything was different now.

They weren't coming quick enough. I knocked again. "Addy, open up!" The keys twisted in my hand as I searched for the right one.

*Where is it? Where is it?*

As I found it and moved to lift it to the lock, the door swung open. My wife stood in front of me, sopping wet with a baby blue towel wrapped around her body and a scowl on her face. A puddle of water droplets was forming around her feet. "What the hell are you doing?" She put a hand on her chest, letting out a gasp of breath. "I thought you were the police, that something had happened to Rory. Jesus, Wes. What's the emergency? What are you doing here?"

"Do you have something to tell me?" I demanded, my body trembling with rage.

"What are you talking about?"

"Do you have something to tell me?" I repeated.

"For heaven's sake, come inside. You're letting all the heat out." She stepped back, but I didn't move.

*"Do. You. Have. Something. To. Tell. Me."* I spat the words

out, more a statement than a question, my eyes drilling into hers.

"I have no idea what you're talking about..." She shook her head, her mouth gaped open.

"I know about the man."

She blinked rapidly at me, her face pale. "What are you talking about? What man?"

"The man you had here today."

For a moment, it looked as though she was going to deny it. Perhaps that's what I hoped would happen. If she denied it, maybe I could go on denying it a little while longer. "Wait a second, are you talking about Matt? How in the world did you know he was here today?"

"Who the *hell* is Matt?" I demanded, still shaking. I refused to answer her questions until she answered mine.

She put up her hands. "Calm down. You've got it all wrong, okay?" She stepped back, gesturing that I should come into the house. "Let me dry off, and I'll explain everything. I'm freezing standing here with the wind blowing in." She shivered, as if to prove her point.

I followed her inside, my anger dissipating only slightly as she shut the door and walked off in a huff, mumbling to herself. I stood near the door, not moving until she reappeared moments later, dressed in her pajamas with her hair wrapped in a microfiber towel atop her head.

"Okay," she said, both hands resting on her hips. "Now then, *Matt*, the man who was here today, is Brody's father, the boy who Rory is dating."

"Oh," I said, letting what she'd said sink in. I felt incredibly foolish as my anger rushed away as quickly as it had arrived. "Oh… Well, why was he… How did you… Why was he here in the middle of the day?"

"Because he's a realtor and his schedule is hectic, but he wanted to meet us."

"Okay, and with *us* being the operative word there, why wasn't I invited?"

"It was last minute. Rory asked if she could go on her first date with this boy. I knew you'd want to meet him first, so I told her as much, and that we'd want to meet his parents—*parent.* His mom passed away a few years ago, so it's just Matt. Anyway, he had an unexpected break in his schedule today and asked if he could come by. Apparently he's just as nervous about Brody dating as we are about Rory. He said he's had a really hard time putting himself out there since his mom died." She paused. "I'm sorry you weren't able to be here. He was supposed to let me know about a day and time soon, but he called me around lunchtime and asked if he could swing by for an hour during his break. I didn't see the harm. I had Tina cover my class for an hour and swung by the house. And, of course, I told him I'm sure you'll still want to meet him. I haven't told Rory that she can date him for sure, but she really likes him and I'm trying to give her a little bit of extra leash."

I stared at her in shock, feeling sick to my stomach. "She's not old enough to be dating. We agreed about that. And you should've called me. Even if I couldn't have made it, you should've let me know that it was happening. You should've given me the option of being here."

"We still aren't in a great place, Wes. And I told you, I didn't have the time to call you."

"You had the time to kiss him," I argued, my jaw tight.

She laughed, slapping her thigh. "Kiss him? Where are you getting this information?"

"That doesn't matter. Are you denying it?"

"Have you been spying on me?" she asked, her brows furrowed.

"Answer the question, Addy. Did you or did you not kiss him?"

"No, I didn't, for the record. I mean, sure, I might've kissed him on the cheek when he left. I was being friendly when he hugged me. It was nothing. He's a really sweet guy going through a hard time."

"How can you be sure he's such a sweet guy? You've only just met him."

She folded her arms across her chest. "Does it matter? Why are you so angry about this? We're both going to be meeting Brody before we make a decision about her dating him."

"When?"

"I haven't heard yet. Rory is supposed to be letting me know."

"Well, I want to meet *Matt*, too."

"Fine," she said stiffly. "Whatever you say."

"And I don't want him over here when I'm not home. I don't like that." Indignant rage swelled in my chest. I hated Matt. I hated everything about him without knowing a single thing about him.

She jerked her head back in shock, her jaw tight. "I don't really think it matters what you like or don't like, Wes."

"What the hell is that supposed to mean?"

"We're separated. What I do is none of your business. He's Rory's boyfriend's dad, for crying out loud. Is this how you're going to react when I start seeing other people?"

My jaw fell open, and I stared at her, in total shock that she'd just said those words. "*When* you start seeing other people? As in you already have your mind made up that you will?"

"I'm not going to turn into a spinster after the divorce, if that's what you were hoping for." She spun around, walking away from me and into the living room, and I followed close behind.

"Actually, I was hoping we could avoid the divorce entirely, if you want to know the truth."

She waved a hand over her shoulder, sounding exhausted as she spoke. "I can't do this with you right now, Wes. I can't fight with you."

"Are you seeing other people, Addy? I deserve to know the truth."

"I'm not seeing other people," she said quickly. "Of course I'm not. I would never cheat on you. I care about you too much for that and you know it. But I will see other people eventually. When this is all over. And you should, too. We both deserve to find happiness, even if that's with someone else. That's what a separation is. That's what a divorce is." She stopped, huffing out a heavy breath. "We're getting a divorce, Wes. I'm going to file the paperwork in a few weeks. You need to prepare yourself. This is happening."

She waited, as though she thought I was going to react, but I didn't. I stayed still, emotionless, trying to process what she was saying. I'd gone from irate to heartbroken in a matter of minutes and my mind still needed time to comprehend it all. "Is that what you really want?" I asked finally, my voice soft.

"It's what I need." She grabbed a throw pillow, holding it at her waist. "I can't—" She tossed it back at the couch with force. "I can't do this anymore with you. I can't keep trying and trying for nothing to work. I can't pretend we're the people we used to be."

I took a step back, my throat tight. "I guess that's that, then."

She nodded. "I want you to be happy, Wes. It's all I've ever wanted."

Another step. I couldn't catch my breath. I needed oxygen. I needed to get out of the house. "Okay," I managed to say.

"I'm sorry."

Bitter tears blurred my vision. "No need to be sorry. You're just being honest, right?"

"Wes, I—"

I turned from her, making my way to the door, then onto the sidewalk and to my car in seconds. She stood in the doorway, watching me as I drove away. I hardly recognized her anymore.

I hardly recognized myself.

## CHAPTER EIGHTEEN

I lay in bed, watching the fan spin overhead. Elias had been in a few times to check on me, but I'd barely acknowledged him. When people say that they have a broken heart, I'd always assumed it was hyperbole, but now, I knew better. I thought I'd had my heart broken before, but it had felt nothing like this. That was truly how I felt—as if something inside of me had broken. Something had snapped beyond repair, and no amount of booze or bad TV or time would ever be able to fix it.

I was broken.

She had broken me.

And I didn't care about picking up the pieces.

*Tick, tick, tick.*

The fan spun around, the metal chain clinking against the glass bulb covers.

*Tick, tick, tick.*

What had she done?

*Tick, tick, tick.*

Why had she given up on us?

*Tick, tick, tick.*

Why wasn't I worth fighting for?

*Tick, tick, tick.*

Was I so easy to give up on?

The door to my room opened again, and I flicked my gaze down. Elias stood there, studying me.

"It was bad, huh?" he said simply.

I gave a jerked nod.

"Is she cheating on you?"

One shoulder gave way to a shrug.

"I'm sorry, man. I really am. Do you wish I hadn't told you?"

I sniffled, wiping a stray tear as it dripped down into my hairline. "It wasn't what you thought," I said. "But it could've been. Next time, it could be."

"What do you mean?" He took a step toward the bed.

"It's officially done," I said. "She's going to start the process."

"Divorce?" he confirmed.

I met his eye, giving an answer without saying a word.

He huffed out a heavy breath. "Well, at least you know now, right?"

"I wish I didn't," I croaked.

"You don't mean that."

But I did. I did mean it because even living a lie was easier than this. "I just want to be alone, man. Please."

He took a step back, departing without another word. I closed my eyes, listening to the whirring of the fan and trying to force my brain to stop producing thoughts. Everything was a challenge. A drain on resources I couldn't afford to use. I needed to rest, but I couldn't find sleep. Everything just hurt. Everything reminded me of her.

When the door opened again, minutes or hours could've passed. I wasn't sure. I planned to be stern with Elias, to tell him to go away, but when I looked down, the person standing there wasn't Elias at all.

"What are you doing here?" I asked.

Stephanie's face was solemn, yet there was an apology in her eyes. She knew what had happened. "You gave me an extra Coleton Day autograph." One of my newest clients. "I was going to bring it back."

"You can leave it with Elias."

She made her way across the room anyway, sitting down on the bed. She didn't say anything, just put a hand on my chest and lay down beside me. Together, we stared up at the ceiling. She smelled nice, like warm vanilla or something baking. It was different than she'd smelled last night. Not better or worse, but different.

I felt her hand slide down my arm, felt her lace her fingers through mine. When she looked at me, I turned my head without thinking and met her eyes. She blinked slowly. There was an understanding there. A question.

I closed my eyes, nodding slightly, then became still as a tear slid down my cheek. Before I could open my eyes, I felt her release my hand, felt the bed shift and heard it squeak as she rolled over on her side. She tossed her leg over my stomach, put a hand on the back of my neck, and pressed her lips to mine.

I didn't shy away, didn't stop her as her kiss grew deeper. Then, I felt myself responding. I kissed her harder, faster, lifting my hand to the back of her neck and pulling her closer to me. My body grew warm with desire as her body pressed into mine.

I felt every moment of the passion, as real and familiar as it had ever been, but it was different somehow. Different with her. It was as if I were watching it happen on TV, our bodies melded together, our lips parting, tongues exploring. Almost as if I was no longer in control of my body, as if I were floating somewhere up above watching it transpire.

I watched as I ran my fingers through her hair, tugging on the dark strands playfully as I nipped at her neck before pulling her on top of me. I watched as she took her shirt off, then mine. I didn't stop her as she reached for my belt, nor did I stop her as she trailed kisses down my stomach.

My tears continued to blur my vision, anger, sadness, and desire fighting for my attention as she pulled my pants toward my ankles before removing her own. My thoughts screamed at me that it was wrong, but I was incapable of stopping it. I didn't want to stop it. I was incapable of doing anything but watching, still floating up above when we were both suddenly stripped of our clothes. Still floating as she sank down on top of me, and I felt myself moving within her, felt her nails digging into my chest. My body moved without volition, desire controlling it completely as I watched it happen mind-lessly, our bodies writhing under the sheets, a steady stream of tears on my cheeks. I was still floating up above as she kissed away those tears, keeping a steady rhythm as she moved on top of me slowly, running a hand through her hair as her breasts bounced hypnotically.

Still floating as I watched her head fall back with ecstasy, her movements slowing for moments, then quickening all at once.

Still floating up above as my vision blurred and leg muscles tightened from my own release moments later.

When it was over, my body exhausted and raw, I felt like I'd been torn open. I felt broken. It was so real and so dreamlike all at once. I cried some more, the once-silent tears turning into outright sobs, and Stephanie wrapped her arms around me, allowing me to fall to pieces on her chest. What had I done? Why did it hurt so badly? She stayed with me as my sobs lulled me to sleep. Just the two of us, our breathing meshing together with the slow, steady hum of the fan.

*Tick, tick, tick.*

# CHAPTER NINETEEN

When I awoke, I was naked and cold. I looked down at my bare body, laying on top of the sheets. I jerked upright, looking around the room. The door to the bedroom was cracked, but Stephanie was gone.

When had she left?

Had it all been a dream?

I stood up and flicked on the lamp on my bedside table, searching for my boxers. I found them at the foot of the bed and pulled them on quickly. Then, I looked around the room with one eye closed, still half asleep.

Where was my phone?

I spied it sticking out from under the bed and picked it up. It was nearly three in the morning, and my battery was on twelve percent. I rubbed the sleep from my eyes, trying to make sense of my screen as I simultaneously tried to plug it in. I had three missed calls and a voicemail from my boss.

Before trying to return his call at such a late hour, I

pressed the button to play the voicemail and listened carefully.

"Wes, hey, it's Stewart. I'm sorry to call so late. Listen, the venue for the platinum party for Layla has had a plumbing leak, and they aren't going to be able to have it fixed in time for the party tomorrow night. I know it's last minute, but your house has always been such a nice space for entertaining. I'll be out of town, so I can't have it at mine. Is there any way you could throw something together quickly? If not, I need you to find a new venue today for me. I know it's tough, but I'm sure you can do it. Anyway, I'm about to board a flight, so I won't be available until tomorrow afternoon. I'll call to check in then. Remember, the party's supposed to be at nine. Once you get everything in order, just give the details to Rodney, and he'll make sure the right people know. Thanks a million, Wes." The voicemail ended, and I stared at my screen. He'd left the voicemail at just past eleven the night before, which meant the party was that evening. I had no house, a broken heart, and a huge problem.

Jumping into action, I grabbed my laptop from its bag on top of the dresser and began searching for venues. It was a much-needed distraction from the current inner turmoil I was dealing with.

I called every single place around town, including several restaurants. Most places didn't answer, and wouldn't for several hours, and the ones that did, didn't have any space or availability to throw together a last-minute party.

I needed to know how many people to expect, and Rodney wasn't answering my calls. I'd estimated around one hundred and fifty, as that was about typical for one of our celebrations, but if I severely over or underbooked, it could end up a disaster.

My heart raced as I searched for answers, jotting down notes. Who was the caterer? Who was in charge of decorating? Was the label delivering the award, or did I need to arrange for it to be picked up? I needed to speak with my boss, but he was somewhere over the Atlantic Ocean with no means of communication for the next several hours. There was no way I was going to call Addy to ask about using the house.

Not a chance in hell after the fight we'd just had, and especially if it would mean facing her after what I'd done... I forced the thought away. It was too painful, which meant I had to figure something else out.

And I would, even if it took all morning.

By six, that seemed to be exactly what was going to happen, as I was quickly running out of options. When I heard footsteps padding across the hardwood floor, I wished I'd shut the door, but it was too late. Elias was standing in my doorway in a matter of seconds, wearing boxers and a white T-shirt. He yawned, rubbing a fist over his eyes.

"What's going on? Did I hear you talking?"

"Sorry, I was on the phone. I didn't mean to wake you up."

"It's okay. I thought you might be looking for Stephanie. She left for her shift a little after midnight."

"Oh," I said, not realizing he'd known she'd stayed over. I assumed he knew the rest of it, too, but I wasn't going to ask. To my relief, he didn't seem as though he was planning to tease me or make me feel guilty about it.

"Are you all right?"

I didn't know if he was talking about because of Addy, or Stephanie, or because I was up and on the phone at six a.m. "Yeah, I'm fine. Just a little stressed. Work emergency," I said, looking back at my screen.

"Anything I can help with?"

"Not unless you happen to have an in with a venue on the shortest notice possible."

"What sort of *in*?"

"We had an issue with a venue for a party that's supposed to be tonight, and I'm supposed to reschedule it and shift everything to a new location by nine o'clock, ideally in time to get the new details out to everyone. Only problem is, everything's booked all across town. Even the bingo hall said no." I gave a sarcastic groan. "My boss wants me to do it at my house, which I ordinarily would, but I can't face her right now." I didn't need to explain whether that was because of our fight or because of what I'd done, and it was a good thing, because I didn't know the answer. "I have no idea what I'm going to do." I ran my hands through my hair feverishly.

"I actually might have something that will work," Elias said, drawing my attention back to him.

"You do?"

"I'll have to call and check, but you remember me saying my friend owns this building? Well, it's actually Garth. And, if I'm not mistaken, there's an old ballroom downstairs that used to be used for events, but now I'm pretty sure it's just used for storage. How many people will you need space for?"

I was still processing the fact that Garth, the quiet, immature gamer owned a building that was worth several million dollars. "Are you serious?"

"Yes," he said, yawning again. "I mean, you could fit a couple hundred in there probably. It's the entire bottom floor of the building, but it's going to need a major scrub down. I'm sure he'll cut you a deal, especially since you'd have to hire the cleaners yourself. But if you need space for more than a couple hundred, I'm not sure..."

"That's perfect, Elias. Perfect. Oh my God, you'd be saving my career. Can you call him?"

He snorted. "Well, he's not going to be happy about being woken up before noon, but I'll see what I can do."

"Thank you. God, thank you. You have no idea how big of a bind I was in."

"Hey, no problem. Helping two of my friends at once here."

"Yes, and tell him we'll pay him whatever he charges, and as soon as he can let us in, I'll have a cleaning crew there."

Elias nodded, clicking his tongue. "Let me get a pot of coffee started, and I'll see what I can get lined up."

"I'll get the coffee," I said, hurrying past him, still dressed in only my boxers. I didn't care. Couldn't. I needed him to dial the number and answer my prayers. He looked at me oddly, and I didn't want to rush him, but I desperately needed him to rush. "It's going to be harder and harder the more time passes. If you can get his permission as soon as possible, I would owe you a huge favor."

"If I keep doing you favors, Wes, you're going to owe me more than you can repay." He winked, walking out of the room and back into his bedroom, leaving me with his words repeating in my head.

Elias had been my saving grace so many times recently, it was true. How would I ever repay him? Better question... What would he want?

# CHAPTER TWENTY

By noon, Garth had finally shown up to unlock the doors to the bottom floor. I was learning that he was the son of real estate developers who had given him the building for his eighteenth birthday.

Apparently, it was supposed to be the start of his career following in his father's footsteps. Instead, he'd become a YouTuber who rated video games. According to Elias, the pay was comparable.

The large room was dusty and smelled stale, but I spied the antique tile on the floor and the detailed frames of the windows. It was like a time capsule down there. As if, after the last party, they'd just closed the doors and forgotten the room existed entirely. The tables were still set out, some of them rotten, but most of them still in good shape.

Dust flew in the air whenever anything moved, but that was an easy fix.

Garth walked across the room and flipped on six light switches, making the room buzz with fluorescent lighting, which began competing with the natural light from the oversized windows.

"It's not great," Garth said from across the room, his voice reverberating around us. "But it can be something. It used to be something special to see, in its day. I let it go to shit to piss off my dad more than anything." He tucked his hands in his pockets. "Who knows? Maybe you'll get it cleaned up enough to make me consider renting it out again."

"You should definitely rent it out, Garth. This place is magnificent. You could host weddings here, parties… It could be an excellent extra source of income."

He pulled out a cigarette, lighting it with a scowl. "Eh, I don't really need the money. It's always been more of a headache than anything. Finding someone to deal with everything, deposits…" He waved his hand through the air. "It's a whole thing. Anyway, there's a giant storage closet in the back corner." He pointed in the general direction. "With extra tables and chairs, or space for you to store the tables if you don't need them. I'm not sure what else is in there but help yourself to whatever. *Mi ballroom es su ballroom.*" His thin mustache curled as his lips upturned into a grin.

"Well, this is great. How much will I owe you? I'll have a check cut by the end of the day."

"Eh, I don't know." He inhaled sharply. "Does three thousand sound fair? Being such short notice and all." For someone who didn't need the money, he was certainly fine with asking for quite a bit. Still, it wasn't more than anywhere else would've charged, especially on this short of notice, and it was my only option.

"I'll have the check for you this afternoon after I get to the office. Do you want me to bring it by your place, or—"

"Just give it to Elias," he said. "He'll get it to me."

"Awesome. Thanks, man. You're really saving me here."

"No problem," he said, placing the cigarette between his lips and inhaling deeply. I watched the black end burn orange, ash falling off the end onto the floor. He ran the toe of his tennis shoe over it, creating a dark, black smudge across the white and gold tile. "Anyway, everything should still work. Just let me know if you have any issues." He looked around again. "She's gonna need a good clean. Hope you brought your bleach."

"I've already got a cleaning crew scheduled to be here in an hour. It's a company we've used before, and they'll have it all cleaned in no time. And the caterers will be here to set up at seven."

He nodded, though I could tell he wasn't really listening. "Sounds good, man. Enjoy it." He inhaled the last of the cigarette, tossing it down onto the tile and stamping it out. "Do you need anything else from me?"

"No, I think we're good." The stale stench of cigarette still permeated my nose. "Thanks again."

He nodded at Elias. "Call me if you need anything. I'm going back to bed." With that, he shook Elias' hand loosely, saluted me, and sulked out of the room. The door closed behind him with a loud thud, and Elias looked at me.

"Well, it's not perfect, but it'll do."

"It's amazing. I can't believe you actually had an in with a venue. I underestimated you, Elias." I laughed.

"It happens." He pushed up his sleeves. "Should we get started cleaning?"

I looked around, trying to decide where to start first. "You don't have to help. I know you probably have work to do. I'm going to leave the cleaning to the experts, but I want to get the rotten tables hauled off and everything else put away. We're renting tables, so I may just put these in the storage closet Garth was talking about. It's over there, right?" I looked toward the back corner where Garth had pointed.

"I'm not sure," Elias said. "Somewhere back there, yeah."

There were doors on every wall, though I had no idea where most of them led, and I had no desire to call the owner back and ask him. Instead, I'd get to exploring, but first things first, I needed to get to the office to get the check and give the updated information to Rodney.

"Okay, cool. Well, I'm going to run across town and get things situated at the office, and then I'll be back to meet the cleaners. Thank you again, man."

"Are you sure you don't need help with anything?"

"You've done more than enough," I told him, patting his shoulder as I walked from the room. "See you tonight."

---

By the time seven that evening rolled around, I was actually starting to think I'd be able to pull the miracle off. The room had been scrubbed from top to bottom, rotting tables and chairs replaced with brand-new ones, and though I hadn't seen it before, I felt confident saying the room had been brought back to its former glory.

The caterers were due to arrive at any moment, and I was jittery with excitement that it had actually worked. When I'd spoken with Stewart in the early afternoon, he'd been positively chipper at the news, overjoyed that I'd found a space and handled everything so efficiently. We'd heard back from about seventy percent of the guest list that they'd still be able to make it to the new location.

I didn't want to jinx anything just yet, but things were certainly starting to feel okay.

When I heard a knock on the door, I looked back, expecting to see the caterers. Instead, Elias walked in the room, looking around with wide eyes.

"Wow. This place really is incredible. I can't believe all of this was under such a thick layer of dust."

"Yeah, it cleaned up well, don't you think?"

He inhaled deeply through his nose. "It doesn't even smell musty anymore."

"Yeah, they've had the exterior doors open most of the day, which seems to have helped."

He smiled, approaching the tables and running his finger over them as if he was checking for more dust.

"Those are all new tables we rented out, so they're perfectly clean."

"Yeah, I thought so."

I had no idea why I was explaining anything to him, but I also had no idea what he wanted. He continued to pace the room, examining everything thoroughly. Finally, he spun around on his heels, his hands clasped in front of his waist.

"So, when does the food get here? I'm starving."

My jaw dropped, and I tried to quickly recover. "Oh, um…" The cheerful, innocent grin on his face made it harder for me to tell him what I needed to. "Well, they'll be here any minute."

"Good," he said quickly, rubbing his hands together hungrily. "I haven't eaten all day. What are we having?"

"We…I'm not sure, actually. My boss approved the menu."

"Ahh, well, something good, I'm sure."

"Listen, Elias, I know you did me such a solid by making sure I found this place on extremely short notice. I can't thank you enough for that. And, while it's no problem for you to grab a plate and take it back upstairs, I'm sure you understand that the party is guest list only, and I don't have a way to bring any guests."

He nodded along as I spoke but stopped when he seemed to understand what I was saying. "Oh, I didn't realize it was so exclusive."

I winced. "Yeah, I mean, I'd love to have you here, trust me. But you know how celebrities are. They want things their way, and we have to keep them happy to keep getting paid, so…" I trailed off. "I'm really sorry."

"You really think they'd mind if just one more person came?"

"I'm sorry, I really do. I just can't control it. I wish I could."

"Oh, okay then. Not a problem. I understand. It's not like you can control it, like you said."

I breathed a sigh of relief, my hand on my chest. "I

wish I could. Trust me. Any other time, you'd be the first one I invited."

"Yeah, I guess I was just thinking since I found you the place, it would be okay, but… I get it."

"I'm really sorry."

"Not a problem," he said. "I get it." His response was curt, and I knew I'd upset him. "Well, let me live vicariously through you anyway. Who's the party for?"

I shouldn't tell him, I knew, but I wanted him to be happy with me again. "Layla O'Neil," I said, regretting it the moment the answer left my lips.

"Oh, wow." He tucked his hands behind his back.

"Yeah…"

"So, she's the one that would approve me to stay, then?"

"Yeah, but she wouldn't," I warned.

"How do you know? Couldn't you just ask her?"

"Elias, it's not like that. These celebrities…they don't really like for strangers to attend their parties."

"But what if you told her I'm a fan?"

"She still wouldn't like it. I'm sorry. I have to follow the rules she gave Stewart. I know you understand."

"I understand," he said with a sly smile. "What a bitch."

He let out a shrill laugh, and I forced a grin. "Yeah, it sucks."

"Well, I know you can't help it. Maybe next time the party will be for someone nicer."

"Yeah, maybe…"

"Or maybe you could talk to Stewart about it, since I did you such a favor tonight."

I started to answer, but at that moment, the door

opened again and I saw the caterers beginning to arrive, filing in carrying in covered trays of food, warmers, and empty serving platters. Once I'd greeted them and pointed them in the direction of the small kitchen area where they could set up, they got to work, and I returned my attention to Elias.

"Are you heading back upstairs? I've gotta run and get a shower before the party. I feel disgusting."

He shook his head. "No, I'm going to grab a plate of food and head out. I guess I'll go to Mac's to game for the evening."

"Ah, okay," I said, feeling guilty. I knew I'd upset him, but I just didn't have the time to fix it at the moment.

*Add it to my ever-growing list of things I need to find a way to fix.*

I also really didn't like the idea of leaving him alone with the caterers, but he seemed in no hurry to leave. "Well, I'll see you later tonight, then. Make sure to leave right after you make your plate, okay? They still need to get everything set up."

"Yep. I've got it," he said. "Sounds good. Have fun tonight."

He turned away from me, returning to pacing the floor awkwardly, as a child would do when their parents were nearly done with dinner. I left the room, hurrying up the eight flights of stairs to our apartment. I opened the door and went inside, locking it behind me as I stripped out of my clothes.

I was starting to feel grimy after a day of running errands and working too hard. I needed a quick shower to refresh and then to get dressed in clean clothing. Layla was one of our more difficult clients, and her staff were picky about everything. I wanted to get downstairs to double-check that everything was in order before the party began. As I turned on the water, I couldn't help wondering just when I'd signed up for a job as an assistant. Normally, this type of thing would be so far outside of my problem, but Stewart had asked, and I'd jumped into action without thinking. I'd have to do better about setting boundaries; it was where the problems with Addy had started in the first place.

*Addy.*

Just the thought of her sent pangs of guilt, heartbreak, and anger radiating to my core. I stepped into the shower, moving under the low-pressure stream of water.

As I shampooed, I closed my eyes and went through a mental checklist of things I'd needed to do that day, crossing them off one by one.

Suddenly, my eyes jerked open. I'd heard something.

*Footsteps.*

Someone was in the apartment.

I'd locked the door behind me when I'd come in…hadn't I?

I couldn't be sure. I thought I had, but there'd been so much on my mind it was entirely possible I'd forgotten to. I lowered my hands from my hair, staying still as I tried to focus. Perhaps I'd imagined it.

After a few moments, I began shampooing again, convinced it had been a noise outside of the apartment, but within minutes, I heard another noise.

*Clang.*

*More footsteps.*

*Shuffling around.*

Someone was in my bedroom.

I stuck my head under the water, rinsing the remnants of the shampoo as quickly as possible, not daring to close my eyes. My heart thudded in my chest as I moved the shower curtain slightly, terrified to make any noise. I left the water running as I stepped out of the shower and pulled my pants back on, my body still soaking wet.

There was nothing in the bathroom that could've been used as a weapon, not scissors or a hair dryer or anything remotely threatening. I'd left my phone outside on the bed. I opened the drawer slowly, cursing myself as I reached with a shaking hand and took hold of my hairbrush. It was all I had, and I knew that wasn't saying much. I placed my ear near the door carefully, attempting to listen. I needed to figure out where the intruder was, so I could decide when to come out.

My heart pounded as I listened to the silence. What if they were waiting just outside of the door? What if they were on the ground, looking at my toes under the door? I scooted them back cautiously. What if they had a gun and they placed it to the door, aligning it with my head?

I couldn't wait any longer. I jerked the door open, holding my breath as I prepared for an attack.

The room was empty.

I released the breath, looking around.

*What the—*

*Buzz. Buzz. Buzz. Buzz.*

I followed the sound, lowering the hairbrush as I realized my phone was vibrating from somewhere in the room. I'd tossed it onto the bed when I came into the room, but it was no longer there. The floor vibrated slightly under my feet, and I knew it must've fallen to the floor.

My throat tightened as the thought that someone could be hiding under the bed, waiting for me to lift the cover, filled my head.

Briefly, I considered running out of the room, but I imagined myself either slipping from the puddles of water near my feet or running straight into the intruder outside. I couldn't slow my racing pulse, couldn't steady my breathing. I bent forward, grabbing the blanket's edge and lifting it into the air with one swift motion. The phone lay facedown on the floor, buzzing in a circle on the hardwood. To my great relief, it was the only thing under the bed.

I picked it up, staring at the screen.

It was Addy, but I had no desire to speak to her.

Finally, it was I who would be ignoring her messages. She'd get a taste of her own medicine. I hit the button to decline the call, noticing that she'd already called two times. Realizing that must've been what I'd heard, that the phone's vibrating must've caused it to fall from the bed, and I'd heard the resulting crash and vibrations from the next two calls left me feeling less on edge.

The tension dissipated from my shoulders, my heart returning to a semi-normal pace, although now, my newest stress was what Addy wanted.

As much as I wanted to be like her and ignore the call, as I made my way back into the bathroom, I realized that something could be wrong with Rory. I couldn't spend the night wondering.

I unlocked the phone, spying a text message as it came in.

My breathing hitched as I read it.

*What the—*

The message contained just two simple words, but I had no idea why she'd directed them at me.

**Fuck you.**

# CHAPTER TWENTY-ONE

Addy was ignoring me once again as I dialed her number, listening to the rings and then her voicemail greeting. I'd texted her back, asking what was wrong, but there had been no reply.

Apparently, I'd done something.

Unquestionably, I had, but the question was *what*. And how did she know whatever it was she knew? Why wouldn't she answer my calls?

I ran gel through my damp hair, rubbing my hands over the stubble on my chin. I needed to shave, but I just didn't have the time. If Addy was mad at me, it meant Rory wasn't hurt, so I was less on edge, but still, her anger was bothering me. I worried that she'd somehow found out about Stephanie and me, but I knew it was impossible.

Forcing myself to focus on the task at hand, I chose one of my two suits that remained hanging in the closet, reminding myself that I needed to pick up the third from the dry cleaners soon, and got myself dressed, my mind racing. I needed to get to the party, host the hell out of it, figure out what was going on with Addy, hope that I hadn't made Elias too angry, and decide what to do about Stephanie.

Once I was dressed, I spritzed on cologne, checking myself out in the mirror one last time before shutting off the bathroom light and then my bedroom light on the way out the door. I checked my phone one last time, just to be sure Addy hadn't called, but I knew she hadn't.

I didn't have time to deal with it. Addy had caused me enough heartache. If she was going to leave me, I had to be sure the one good thing left in my life—my career—was taken care of. After what I'd pulled off today, I'd already decided I was going to ask Stewart for a promotion. God knew I deserved it.

I made my way out of the apartment—triple checking that I'd locked the door—and down the stairs, surprised to find that Elias was still in the ballroom. He'd taken a seat at one of the tables, a half-eaten plate of food in front of him.

It was after eight, which meant that any moment now, people would start arriving. I needed to get him out of there. Even if Stewart wasn't adamantly against having friends or family at work or work functions, Elias was embarrassing. I hated to think it so plainly, but I didn't want him to start acting weird again and get me in trouble or humiliate me somehow.

I walked across the room, the temperature a few degrees cooler than I would've liked as a result of poor insulation and concrete walls, and he looked up when he heard my shoes clicking across the tile.

"Hey, bud. Did you get yourself something to eat?" I

stared at the brown barbecue sauce stain on the white tablecloth under his plate. He saw me staring and smiled sheepishly.

"Sorry, I tried to clean it up, but it only made it worse." He lifted the plate, revealing the smear was much worse than it had originally looked. The table he'd chosen was in the center of the room, meant to be the table where Layla sat.

I wrinkled my nose in frustration, trying to think. "It's okay, I just need to swap it out quickly." I pretended to be a lot less panicked than I felt. "Can you move your plate please?" He took too big of a bite from his brisket taco—so much for being a vegetarian—and stood up, holding his plate with one hand while he crunched loudly, getting crumbs everywhere.

I ignored him, my body trembling with anxiety as I whipped the tablecloth from the table and hurried across the room, trading it with a tablecloth from a table in the far back corner. I jogged back across the room, laying the cloth out flat.

"There we go."

Elias went to sit down again, but I shouted, stopping him before he connected with the chair. "Wait!" In the distance, I heard the exterior door in the hall open, and warm voices flooded the floor. My guests had arrived and would be in here any moment, and I was staring at Elias, who had one cheek bulging with food, and his fingernails were stained with barbecue sauce. I tried not to sneer as I looked him over. "You should probably get going, right?" I gestured toward the door that led straight out to the street. "Do you need me to call you an Uber to get to Mac's?"

He grinned playfully. "I can't exactly take this food in an Uber, Wes."

"Well, why don't I try to wrangle you up a to-go box. I'm sure they have one here somewhere."

"I'm almost finished," he argued. "Just let me get done eating, and I'll get out of your hair."

"The party is getting ready to start, the guests are starting to arrive. I can't—"

"Wes!" Rodney called from the doorway. "Can you come help me carry this stuff inside?"

I glanced back at him. "Yeah, just a second."

"Come on, Elias. I need you to leave. We talked about this," I said, keeping my voice low, my eyes pleading with him.

I watched as he licked the sauce from one of his fingers, working his way through all five slowly. When he was finished, he smiled up at me wildly. "Don't worry about me. I know the rules. I'll be gone by nine, just as soon as I finish eating. You won't even know I'm here. Go take care of your guests. I'll sneak out when I'm done."

"I'm not allowed to have you here—"

"Wes, where do you want us to set up?" The DJ, Dalton, walked in, an entire setup crew behind him.

"I—"

"Wes, we really need to get this stuff brought in. Come on, man, I'm double parked," Rodney called with frustration.

"Go on," Elias said plainly, taking a seat at the next

table with a wicked smile on his face. "Sounds like you have work to do. Don't worry about me."

"I—" The entire room was looking at me, and I knew my face must've been pink with anger, but there was nothing I could do. I groaned, walking away from him, my stomach sick with rage. "You can set up in the far corner. There are plug-ins over there," I told Dalton, nodding at Rodney. "Let's go get these. Sorry about that. I'll be right back in," I called to no one in particular and everyone all at once.

Of course, when we came back inside, Elias had not only *not* left, but he was happily chatting with the DJ as he set up his equipment. I groaned, heaving the oversized photo of Layla over the threshold and into the room. I set it up on its easel near the door and helped Rodney unload the rest of the photos of her and the plaque the record label had sent over.

Layla's manager, Justin, came in just as I was making my way across the room to confront Elias.

"Wes!" he called, waving me over. I couldn't seem to catch my breath from all the anger and frustration. This was supposed to be a night of celebration, not only for my client, but for the agency, for the record label, and for myself for getting it all together so quickly. Why was Elias hell-bent on ruining just as much as he fixed for me? I just didn't get him.

Ryan threw an arm around me, whispering in my ear. "Okay, here's the deal: Layla is still good to sing a few songs tonight, but she's dealing with a sore throat, so we were thinking we could keep it low-key, maybe just some acoustic, stripped down songs so she isn't belting, you know?" He looked behind us. "Do we have instruments here?"

"I can get some," I promised, though I had no idea if I could.

"Okay, perfect." He patted my chest and released me. "And keep it between us about the…" He gestured to his throat. "The tour starts next week, and we're keeping all the vibes positive." He crossed both sets of fingers.

I nodded as he walked away from me, and I immediately began searching for Rodney. Just as he zipped past me, I grabbed at his shirt. "Rodney, wait!" He stopped short, out of breath as he buzzed around trying to get everything set up. "I need you to run out and get some equipment."

He looked as exhausted as I felt as I rambled off the instructions. "Go to a music shop on Broadway called Evanston's. Ask for Dan. He's the owner, and he owes me a few favors. We need an acoustic guitar and a keyboard. Tell him it's for me."

Rodney nodded. "We need them tonight? For this? We have the tracks for Layla to perform here already."

"Yeah, there's been a change of plans, and I just found out. Listen, tell Dan I'll get it all back to him tomorrow. Call me if there are any issues. You have my number in your phone?"

He nodded. "Okay, get going then. And thank you." He dashed away from me just as I heard the door opening again and more people beginning to pile in the room, filling the tables and dance floor quickly as the time grew closer to nine.

"What are you doing?" I asked Elias when I got near him.

He looked confused for a second, but then clarity came over his expression. "Oh, sorry, man." He pointed to the clock on the wall. "Look, it's not even nine yet. I got distracted talking to Dalton here. Did you know he's from a place called Booger Hole, West Virginia?" He let out a delighted laugh, clutching his stomach, his cheeks bright red. "Can you imagine? Booger Hole? *Where are you from? Oh, I'm from Booger Hole.*" He let out another scream of laughter, echoing through the room.

"Elias, please!" I begged. "This is my job. You *can't* be here right now. I'm begging you."

"He's not botherin' me," Dalton said. "If that's what you're worried about."

Elias looked at me defiantly, and I nodded at Dalton, then put a hand on Elias' shoulder and led him away so we could talk privately. "What's going on? You promised me you'd leave when you finished eating. Why are you doing this to me? Do you want me to get fired?"

"Of course not, bud," he said. "I'm sorry. I just got carried away. I really don't want you to get into trouble. I'm just so mesmerized by it all. I've never gotten to attend a fancy Hollywood party."

"This isn't a Hollywood party. It's an agency party for one of our clients, and the guest list is closed, like I told you. You need to leave, Elias. *Now.*"

"I will, I will," he teased, patting me on the shoulder as he walked past me in no hurry whatsoever. "Jeez, Mom. Hold your horses."

I took off after him, just as one of the waitstaff approached me, stopping me in my tracks. "I'm sorry to interrupt. My boss wants to know if you'd like us to move ahead and start filtering through the room with hors d'oeuvres or if you'd prefer that we wait until exactly nine."

At her question, another rambunctious group entered the room. I recognized the drummer from Layla's band, his arms around the women on either side of him. "Sorry," I said, drawing my attention back to her. "Yeah, you can go ahead and start. We have," I checked the time, "ten or so minutes. Maybe start with the drinks… Whatever your boss thinks."

She nodded affirmatively and walked away from me, disappearing into the kitchen. Once she was gone, I searched the room for Elias again, having lost him in the ever-growing crowd.

Just as I spotted him, on the far side of the room talking with Oliver and two of the interns from work, I heard loud clapping. A round of applause grew, and I looked back at the door, where I saw Layla standing, two of her bodyguards taking their places by the door while another kept a few paces behind her.

She stood there, one arm tucked in front of her stomach, the other folded behind her back as she feigned humility, shaking her head politely at the growing applause. When it began to die off, she offered a slight bow and a pageant-wave before making a beeline toward a group of people, her manager in tow.

I needed to find Elias. I had to get rid of him, and quickly, before he had a chance to do anything awful. As I zigzagged through the crowd, my phone began to ring, and I hoped, despite the chaos, that it would be Addy.

As I pulled it out of my pocket, trying to keep my eyes trained on Elias, I glanced down just once to see it was Rodney who was calling. "Hello?"

"Would you like some champagne?" a waiter asked, holding out a tray for me. I waved him off as politely as I could.

"Dan isn't here, and no one else here knows you. What do you want me to do?" Rodney asked.

I groaned, running a hand over my face. "Okay, did you tell them it's for Layla? You have a business card on you, don't you?"

"Yeah, but they wouldn't budge. The guy said they can't make those decisions, and they tried to call Dan, but he didn't answer. I guess he's out of town."

"Shit," I cursed under my breath. Elias left the group he'd been talking to, circulating through the crowd as if he knew everyone there. He stopped a waiter and took a glass of champagne from the silver tray. "Okay. I'll…I'll figure something else out. Just come on back."

"Okay, see you in a bit."

I ended the call, trying to relocate Elias or Layla's manager, Justin, whoever I could find first. My stomach dropped when I found them at the same time, Elias standing in the small circle that Layla had joined, talking to her animatedly.

I moved in closer, my heart pounding. I was going to lose my job. It was all I had left, and Elias was going to take it from me.

"Hey!" I said, forcing a smile as I joined the group. "What are we talking about?"

"Oh, nothing, roomie," Elias said, downing the glass of champagne in his hand and reaching for another as a waiter walked past. "I was just telling Layla what a big fan I am."

"I'm sure Layla has plenty of mingling to do, Elias. Could I talk to you for a minute?"

"I'm fine here," he said plainly, looking back down at Layla, who smiled uncomfortably. "So, which was your favorite city to play in?"

"Hey," Justin said, "are we all good to go?" He put both his thumbs up.

I shook my head. "I'm still trying to find something. My connection is out of town."

Layla looked concerned from behind her speckled golden eyeshadow. She didn't answer Elias' question, her attention focused solely on us. "What's wrong?" She looked at Justin, whose face was instantly soothing.

"Nothing. We're tracking down some equipment for your performance tonight. I don't want you to worry about it. We've got you taken care of." He wiggled a finger at me, pulling me away from the group, though I desperately didn't want to leave Elias there.

"Listen," he said, once we were out of earshot. "She can't do acapella, because it'll show off the breaks in her voice, but if you can just get a guitar here, I'm sure Will or Tony will be fine to play. So, don't worry about the player, just find the guitar."

"That's just it," I said, keeping an eye on Elias, on high alert every time he leaned down to whisper something to

Layla, which was growing to be more frequent. "I'm looking for a guitar, but I don't have one. Do you think any of the guys has one with them?"

He tensed his lip. "I can check. Stewart told me you were handling everything, Wes. If I'd known I needed to bring instruments, I would've."

It felt unfair, being that I'd just been told I needed to find them as well, and it did seem like he'd had much more warning than me, but I didn't argue. "It's fine. I'll get it figured out. Don't worry."

"You sure?" he asked, his brows raised.

Elias' obnoxious laugh echoed through the room over the soft music Dalton had begun playing.

"Wes?" Justin asked again.

"Yeah, yes," I confirmed.

"Okay, cool." With that, he walked away, and I pulled out my phone again. This time, Addy was calling. I ignored the call, immediately regretting it, and dialed Rodney.

"Hey, I'm just pulling in."

"I need you to go back," I said.

I could hear the frustration in his voice. "Why?"

"I just need you to buy a guitar. Do you have the company card?"

"Yeah," he said.

"Okay, cool. Tell them you need a used one with new strings and you need them to tune it for you before you leave."

"Okay," he said with a heavy sigh.

"Thanks, Rodney."

I ended the call just as Addy's name appeared on my

screen again. Torn between trying to chase down Elias again and answer the call, I pressed the phone to my ear, scanning the room. I was out of breath when I answered.

"Hello?"

"How could you do this to me?" she asked. I knew right away that she was crying, her sobs making it hard to understand her. "You made me feel like crap because I had Rory's boyfriend's dad over for a half hour to get to know him for our daughter. Meanwhile, you're sleeping with another woman."

My stomach fell, a lump forming in my throat as my skin instantly chilled at her words. *No.* I pressed a finger to my opposite ear, Elias momentarily forgotten, and rushed out of the room. "What are you talking about?"

"The picture, Wes. Don't play stupid with me. You obviously were trying to prove a point, and you've done that. I can handle a lot of things from you, almost everything, but I wasn't prepared for you to be outright cruel to me… Who was she? Was she even someone you knew? Or just…some random woman you picked up at a bar? I was trying to be kind to you… Throughout all of this, I've tried to be mindful of your feelings. I know that you may not agree with my decision to move forward with the divorce, that you were hurt by it, but I would never purposefully hurt you. I thought we were better than that."

She was sobbing as she spoke, her words coming out in garbled clumps and then several inhales before the next phrase. I was having to work to understand what she was saying, but I caught the gist. How did she even know? I hated myself for hurting her, for causing these tears. This was never what I wanted.

"Addy, I wasn't trying to hurt you. You told me you were going to see other people and I—" I lowered my voice as a group of people walked past me. "I was devastated. I *am* devastated. I'm an idiot. It was a mistake. You broke my heart, and I just—I don't want to lose you. I don't want a divorce."

"Yeah, well, that's one hell of a way to show it, Wes. It's bad enough that you did it at all, but I can't fault you, because you're right, I showed you the door. But to send me that picture, I just don't under—"

"Hold on," I said, pressing my finger harder into my ear as I tried to focus on what she was saying. The door to the room swung open as the group entered, momentarily encompassing me in loud music. I headed for the staircase, trying to make sense of her words. "What picture? What are you talking about?"

"Oh, are you seriously going to pretend you don't know?"

"I'm not pretending. I have no idea what you're talking about. Are you honestly saying that you aren't the person who sent a naked photo of you and some random woman to my phone? Honestly, Wes, even if you were just trying to hurt me, Rory could've seen it. Did you even think of that?"

I nearly dropped my phone, looking for my text messages. I clicked on her name, reading the last message from her. Before that, there was nothing. No picture. No outgoing messages. I put the phone back to my ear. Oliver's warning echoed in my ear, my heartbeat echoing in my ears.

"I didn't send you a picture, Addy. I would never do that. You have to know I'm not that person."

"Well who did, then? *The woman?* Why would she do that? Why, Wes? Does she even know who I am?"

I huffed out a heavy breath, trying to think. I could hear my heartbeat in my ears. "I don't understand. So, you got a picture, from my phone, of…"

"Yes." She stopped me from having to fill in the blank.

"Listen, I think someone may have cloned my phone."

"Cloned your—what are you even talking about right now?"

"It's the same thing with the text message to Rory. I never sent it. And I couldn't have sent this one either. I was taking a shower when you started calling. I thought I heard someone in my room. So even if it wasn't a clone, maybe someone broke in or… *Elias.* Elias was mad at me about not inviting him to a party. Maybe he did it. I need to reset my phone. Oliver thinks that may help, but—"

"What are you talking about? What party? Why would Elias take a photo of you and send it to me? And what does any of this have to do with factory resetting your phone? You're not making any sense."

I clenched my fists at my sides. So much about the situation didn't make sense. If someone had cloned my phone, how would they have managed to get a picture of Stephanie and me? And, if it was Elias, how would he have managed to sneak into my room without getting caught and still be down here eating in such a short amount of time? And how would he have had the photo in the first place? "When did you get the picture? When did I send it to you? Around seven thirty?"

"No. You sent it early this morning, right around the time I got to work. Please don't play games with me, Wes. I know it was you, I just don't understand why you would do it. Who was she?" She inhaled sharply, sniffling.

"She was—it doesn't matter. I... Addy, I—"

"No, you know what, I don't want to know. I debated even bringing this up to you. It doesn't even warrant a response, quite frankly. But I've been so upset. I'm so angry with you. I just don't understand."

"Listen to me," I said firmly. "I didn't do this. Do you hear me? I have no idea who did, but I'm going to find out."

She was silent.

"Do you hear me?"

"I just...I don't have time for this, Wes. When you're ready to talk about this like adults, let me know. I have to go."

"Addy, wait—" But the call had ended, and she was gone. I clutched my phone in both hands, concealing a scream. I couldn't calm myself down, the anger that had been bubbling at the surface all night was overflowing, and I had no desire to stop it. I was going to get to the bottom of this. First the text to Rory, then the picture to Addy. Whether my phone had been cloned or Elias was playing a terrible prank, or something more sinister was going on entirely...I had to get it figured out before my life was ruined. Whatever was going on, it was time for answers.

I stormed into the ballroom just as Rodney came in

from the opposite door with a guitar in hand. He made his way toward me, but I ignored him, headed straight for Elias, who had a new glass of champagne in his hand, the dab of barbecue sauce still on his cheek.

When he saw me, his eyes lit up. "Wes, hi!" he waved, calling to me loudly. "Hey, guess what? You were wrong about her. Layla's not bitchy at all. She's so nice!"

The room fell silent, even the music dying out as I stared at him in horror. Layla's jaw dropped, her eyes narrowing at me, and I felt my face growing ashen. I wanted to melt into a puddle right then and there.

"Oops," Elias said, covering his mouth with his pointer finger. "Sorry. Champagne goes straight through me."

# CHAPTER TWENTY-TWO

A few hours later, after the party's sudden conclusion when Layla had stomped out of the room with Justin close behind her, I sat alone on the floor of the ballroom, staring at the dirt in the grout between the tiles.

I couldn't forget the way everyone had stared at me, people who had once respected me, people I greatly admired in the industry. I'd worked my ass off to make the night everything Stewart wanted it to be, and all my hard work had been for nothing.

Layla hadn't even performed or taken her award. I knew by the time she made it home, I would be fired. Not only fired, but word would've spread about me. I'd never be considered hirable again in any circles she ran in. And though the music industry may seem big, I knew the world I worked for was quite small indeed. Disrespecting an artist, ruining a party—either one could be a career ender, but the combination of both was sure to do the trick.

I had no idea why I'd agreed with Elias when he'd said it. Truth was, I didn't even know that I had. I barely even remembered the conversation. I'd just wanted Elias to leave, and going along with him had seemed easiest.

What was I going to do now?

Elias left shortly after his slipup, so quickly that I hadn't had a chance to confront him about the text message. Truth was, I wasn't sure where to even begin with the questions I had for him. I couldn't tell where the anger began and confusion ended. More than anything, I wanted to know why. Why would he do this? What had I done to deserve it?

I sat there, in the quiet, empty room long after everyone had disappeared. I didn't want to face my roommate, or the inevitable truth that I would need to move out and had nowhere to go. And, soon enough, no job to pay for any place I *did* want to go.

As rage bubbled in my belly, I finally summoned up the strength to stand, flipping off the lights as I went out of the room. The stairwell was quiet, my footsteps echoing loudly through the nearly silent building. Once I'd reached the eighth floor, I stared at the door, squaring my shoulders to it.

This was it. The moment of truth.

I stuck my key in the door, almost surprised that it opened—I knew it was illogical, but part of me expected him to have changed the locks before I could get upstairs. When I stepped inside the apartment, the living room was silent and dark. I reached for the switch on the wall, flipping it on.

"Elias? Where the hell are you?" I barked.

At that exact moment, I heard him roar from the bathroom, the unmistakable sound of vomit spewing into the toilet. He coughed, paused, and then I heard it again. My upper lip curled in disgust, and I couldn't bring myself to feel any pity for him. I walked into my bedroom, grabbing the suitcase from the closet and beginning to stuff things inside of it. I'd already thrown away the boxes I'd used to move, but I could take the most important things that night and come back for the rest at some point in the future.

I heard him flush the toilet across the apartment and then listened carefully to his footsteps on the hardwood. I packed quicker, my body trembling with an unsettling combination of fear and rage.

I heard the sound of the refrigerator opening, then heard it shut moments later. When he knocked on my door, I realized it was the first time he'd ever shown that small courtesy.

I didn't answer, continuing to pack, though the suitcase was beginning to get admittedly quite full. After a second knock, he swung the door open slowly, a bottle of water in his hand. His cheeks were pink, from the alcohol or vomiting, I wasn't sure, and he rested his head against the frame of the door.

"You must hate me." He waited for me to correct him, but I didn't bother. "You have no idea how sorry I am."

I hadn't decided what I was going to say to him until the conversation began, but once he'd said that, I stopped packing, slamming my hands onto the piled-up clothing. "Elias, I don't even know where to start. How could you…

Why would you… You probably cost me my job. Do you realize that?"

He blinked slowly, still obviously drunk. "Wes, I never meant to-to hurt you. You're my best friend. I told you I hadn't had anything to eat until dinner, and it just hit me all at once. I wasn't thinking."

"I told you to leave. I told you, you weren't even allowed to be there. You should've left. You shouldn't have been there in the first place."

"I wasn't thinking. You're just so cool. You've always been cool." He hung his head, staring at the water. "Unlike me."

"Oh, please. Don't give me that pity party right now. I worked my entire life to get that job, Elias. My entire life. Years of hard work and late nights, to the detriment of my marriage, and now it's all gone in one night."

"Maybe I can talk to Stewart. He likes me. He'll listen. I can tell him it was my fault. Or maybe I can talk to Layla—"

"*Don't!*" I slammed the lid of the suitcase closed and approached him, wagging my finger in the air. "Don't go near her. Don't you think you've done enough damage? Was this your plan all along? Ruin my life? Why?"

"Ruin your life?" he asked, his jaw hung open, eyes wide in horror. "Wes, you're the best friend I've ever had—"

"I'm not your best friend," I said angrily. "I don't even know you, Elias. And as of right now, I'm not your room-mate either. You've cost me enough."

There were tears in his eyes as he stared at me. "You

don't mean that. You know it was an accident. You know I didn't mean to—"

"Was the text message to Addy an accident, too?"

He shook his head. "What text message to Addy?"

"I know it was you, Elias. I don't know why or-or how, but I know it was you."

"I honestly have no idea what you're talking about."

"What are you, some kind of…psycho? Or are you just out to ruin my life in any way you can? How did you get the picture, Elias? Did you come in and take it while we were sleeping, you sick fuck? Or did you plan it with Stephanie? Maybe she only slept with me because you asked her to."

He jerked his head back. "Wait, you *slept* with Stephanie?" If he was acting, he was certainly convincing.

"Yes, and someone sent a picture to Addy of the two of us." I paused. "It wasn't you?"

"Of course it wasn't. This is the first I'm hearing about any of this. Wes, I'd never…" He put a hand on his stomach. "Oh my God."

"But if not you, then who? Stephanie?"

He shrugged one shoulder halfheartedly. "I have no idea. I knew she stayed with you, but I didn't know you slept together, and I certainly didn't know she sent a text to Addy." He ran a hand over his forehead. "God, I'm so sorry, Wes. What can I do?"

"Nothing," I said quickly. "I don't want your help anymore. Whatever you've done for me has only made my life worse."

He nodded, but it was slow, sad. "I understand. I really

am sorry for…everything. I never meant for any of this to happen. Truly, I just wanted to help you out."

"Well, it's a little late for that, Elias," I cried, feeling hot, angry tears fill my eyes. "Because everything is so fucked up. I don't even…I don't even know what to do." I sat down on the edge of the bed, placing my face in my hands. I didn't know where I was going when I left there. Addy wanted nothing to do with me. I couldn't go to the office. I had my car, and that was it. I'd be officially homeless and jobless the moment I left. That was how quickly it could all change.

I heard Elias approaching me and felt his hand touch my shoulder carefully. "I understand if you don't want to stay here. Honestly, I do. And you're free to go. I know you think I did this stuff on purpose, but trust me, making an ass of myself in front of a celebrity was not on my to-do list for the day. I know you don't believe me, but I've only ever wanted to help you, Wes. I may not be your friend, and I don't blame you for that, but you're still mine. You've been kind to me when I really needed someone, and I wanted to return the favor. I know I didn't succeed, but this was never my intention. I don't know what happened with you and Stephanie, but if she did anything to hurt you, she's not a friend of mine." He paused, removing his hand. "I've never been good with people. It's why my only friends have come through gaming. And then I ran into you, and you were so nice to me. And you had this cool job and this cool life—"

I laughed, interrupting him. "*Cool*, yeah." The sarcastic comment came without warning.

"To someone who sits in front of a screen all day, your life is the coolest. I know I screwed things up for you tonight, but if you'll just let me talk to your boss, tell me what to say, tell me what to do, I promise I'll do it. If not, if you don't think I can, at least let me give you some money for a hotel."

"I don't want your money, Elias."

"What are you going to do, then? Where are you going to go?"

"I don't know… I don't know."

"Stay here," he said softly. "Even if just for the night. I won't talk to you. I won't even leave my room. Just stay here for the night, get some sleep, and you can figure everything out in the morning. I just don't want you to leave with nowhere to go."

I didn't answer, every possible option—and there weren't many—swimming through my head. I needed to talk to Stewart, to explain things before he heard the news from someone else, if he hadn't already. I needed to talk to Addy, too, though what I wanted to say, I had no idea.

The truth was, everything I was mad at Elias for, was my fault. Whether or not he'd sent the text message, I'd been the one to sleep with someone else. Whether or not he'd acted stupidly at the party and insulted my client, I'd been the one to agree with the stupid thing. I couldn't forgive him, but more importantly, I couldn't forgive myself.

Elias stood from the bed suddenly. "Just think on it, okay?" he asked, his voice strained. "I'm going to go throw up."

With that, he was out of the room and I was left alone, exhausted and furious, but with no one to be angry with but myself.

# CHAPTER TWENTY-THREE

Sleep came in waves for me that night. On and off, I'd crash into the abyss, then be brought back just as quickly. I couldn't focus, couldn't even find the energy to change out of my suit or take off my shoes.

I just kept wishing it had all been a bad dream. That I could wake up a few days earlier and get a redo for every bad decision I'd made.

Around six a.m., the text message I'd been expecting from Stewart came in, and with it, a small glimmer of hope.

**My flight lands at 10 a.m. Meet me at the office.**

I pulled the covers over my face, wondering just what he'd been told and how harsh my punishment would be. Was I overreacting? Maybe Layla could be convinced to laugh it off…

…even though she'd been humiliated in front of her band, her friends, and more than a hundred people in our industry.

But at the end of the day, how bad was it really?

Elias had crashed the party, gotten too drunk, and said something stupid. That wasn't exactly a rarity for parties, was it?

Stewart *did* like Elias. Maybe that would help me out somehow.

Or maybe I could say I didn't even know what he was talking about.

That was what I'd tried to yell as she stormed out of the room, stopped from chasing after her by her body-guards. Even if I got her to believe that, who would take me seriously anymore? My coworkers had all watched me embarrass myself beyond belief, ruining a party that was meant to celebrate not only one of our newest clients, but also one of our biggest.

Even if Layla were able to forgive me, there was no way she'd work with us again. I'd have cost the company hundreds of thousands, if not millions of dollars in the long run.

I lay in bed, stewing over how miserable my life had become, for around an hour after the message came in, but finally, I could take it no longer. I stood up, walking out of the bedroom and making my way into the kitchen to fix myself some coffee. If I was going to function at all, I'd need copious amounts of caffeine to do so.

I started the pot of coffee, listening to the quiet hum of the apartment. Even the world outside was quiet at that time of morning. I rested my back against the counter, running a palm over my face as I tried to wake myself up.

It felt as if the past night was a blur, bits and pieces coming back to me as if I'd been drunk, though I was far from it.

Finally, when the smell of coffee hit my nose, I turned around, opening a cabinet and pulling down a mug. I filled the mug, opened the refrigerator, and added creamer, holding the door open with my hip.

Once it was made, I walked back into my bedroom, drinking it as I dug through my suitcase in search of clothes. Everything was wrinkled inside the bag, but I had very little choice, as I'd torn everything from the closet and drawers the night before.

Once I'd chosen something suitable to wear, I downed the last of my coffee and walked into the bathroom. As soon as I picked up my toothbrush, I remembered using the last of the toothpaste the day before. In the whirlwind of everything, toothpaste had been the last thing on my mind.

I weighed my options: I could skip brushing and just use mouthwash for the morning, I could run down to the store on the corner of the street, or I could ask Elias to borrow some. As much as I didn't want to have to ask for his help with anything else, the last option seemed the most appealing.

Holding my toothbrush in one hand, I walked across the apartment and knocked gently on Elias' door. If what he'd said last night was true, maybe he'd be happy to have a small way to make it up to me. Not that this made us anywhere close to even.

"Elias?" I knocked again, when several moments had passed and he hadn't answered.

Still nothing.

I looked behind me, checking to be sure he wasn't on

the couch or sneaking up behind me. "Elias?" I called again.

Having decided he must've run out for something, I clicked my tongue. I didn't want to go into his room without permission, but it wasn't like he'd respected my privacy in any way since I'd gotten there.

If I hurried, I could get in and get a dab of toothpaste without him ever knowing I'd been in there.

Without another thought, I pushed open the door and stepped inside. Immediately, I was hit with a wave of familiar cologne. The warm bergamot notes welcomed me, the scent overpowering as if he'd doused the entire room in it. It was my cologne.

I stepped inside the dark room. There was a bed to my left, its blue and brown plaid comforter askew. A computer desk with two monitors and a gaming keyboard with a headset lying on top of it sat against the exterior wall, the dark screens facing me. The room was messy, clothes thrown about here and there, with an overflowing hamper of laundry in front of the window.

Sharing a wall with the door I'd just entered from was a tall dresser with a few belts, a coffee mug, a half-full bottle of vodka, two empty bags of Twizzlers, and a single bottle of cologne lying on top. I ran a finger over the cap. It was nearly full, but unmistakably mine. Had he taken my cologne? Why hadn't I noticed?

I stepped over a pair of jeans that had been turned inside out, making my way toward the door beside the bed, where I knew his bathroom would be, as our rooms were mirror images of each other. As I reached for it, I glanced at his bed, at the indention where his head would've rested against the pillow last night.

There was something eerie about being in the apartment without Elias. I tried to picture him here. In this room. Living out his days behind the computer screen.

Under the comforter of his bed, something caught my eye, and I took a step closer to the bed, cocking my head to the side as I tried to make sense of it. With a cautious hand, I reached for the edge of the blanket, tossing it back.

Sure enough, the white shirt I'd been looking for two days ago was lying in his bed, crumpled and sweat stained as if he'd been wearing it. But why? And why was it in his bed? I picked it up cautiously.

"What are you doing?" I spun around, the shirt gripped in my hand. Elias was standing behind me, a white plastic sack of candy slung over his forearm. He looked at the shirt in my hand, then at the toothbrush. "Why are you in my room?" It was the first time I'd ever seen him look angry, his nostrils flaring and forehead wrinkling into a scowl.

"Why do you have my shirt?"

"I borrowed it for your party," he said simply. "Before you told me I couldn't come. I don't have any nice clothes."

"No, I was missing this before the party."

"Well, then I guess I borrowed it before. Does it matter?"

"It wasn't yours to take! You didn't even ask me."

"You were busy. I didn't think you'd mind. Is it a big deal?" He nodded toward the toothbrush. "What are you doing in my room in the first place? Why didn't *you* ask *me* if you could come in?"

"I did," I said firmly, then changed my tone slightly. I did still need to borrow something from him, after all. "I mean, I knocked. You didn't answer. I needed to borrow toothpaste."

He walked past me, opening his bathroom door and walking back out seconds later with a tube of cinnamon-flavored toothpaste still in the box. "Keep it. I have extra."

"I just need a little bit."

"I'm weird about germs," he said, though from the look of his room, that was a lie. "Just keep it."

I tucked it under my arm. "Did you borrow my cologne, too?"

His gaze zipped to the bottle of cologne. "No, that was a Christmas present from a few years ago. I rarely use it. Do you use the same kind?"

"Why does the room smell like it, then?"

"I sprayed it this morning to cover up the vomit smell," he said, running his shoe over a pen on the hardwood. "It was rank when I woke up, which is why I left to get cleaning supplies." He gestured to the second bag in his hands, which I could now see contained disinfectant and rags.

He stared at me as if it were the most reasonable explanation, but it just didn't make sense. "Why was my shirt in your bed, then?"

He furrowed his brow. "How should I know? I probably laid it there when I was planning to get dressed, and then I forgot it was there."

"But it's crumpled and sweaty."

"I sweat when I sleep, Wes. What are you implying? You're acting crazy."

"Were you wearing my shirt, Elias? And my cologne? And…and trying to take my job last night, my friends?" I furrowed my brow as the questions filled my mind. It was all too strange to be a coincidence, wasn't it? "What are you doing? Why are you doing this?"

"Oh, yeah. Fine, you caught me." He held his hands up in mock defeat, the white bag swinging wildly as he did. "I put your shirt on and spritzed myself with your cologne, and I lay in bed and pretended to be you because you're just *so* cool, Wes. Slowly but surely I'm going to copy everything you do until we're the exact same person. I mean, who wouldn't want to be you? It's the only reason I invited you here… To learn more about you and take over your life, which is amazing, by the way. You're really on top of the world." He pulled his pants out from his waist, glancing down. "Don't ask me where your favorite boxers are." He batted his eyelashes at me playfully, letting out a laugh.

"It's not funny. Is that what you're doing? Is this all some kind of prank? Because if it is, I swear, I'll—"

"Calm down, man. Has anyone ever told you you're a little paranoid? It's kind of intense…" He yawned, stretching his arms above his head. "Anyway, this has been fun, but I need to get the room cleaned so I can get to work. I have an appointment in a few hours. Do you need anything else?" He held out his hand, gesturing that I should leave. As if I was the intruder. As if I'd weaseled my way into his life and ruined everything.

I was half tempted to lie down on his bed, refusing to

leave as he'd done to me on my first night, but staying in his presence was significantly worse than leaving, even with all the questions burning in my mind, so instead, I sulked away, making my way back to my bedroom. I had more important things to worry about, like saving my job —by some miracle—and getting the hell out of this apartment before I lost my mind. I opened the toothpaste, tossing the box into the small trash can next to my bathroom sink.

Before I opened the tube and brushed my teeth, I checked my underwear drawer, just to be sure my favorite boxers weren't missing after all.

# CHAPTER TWENTY-FOUR

From the moment Stewart walked into the office, I all but knew it was a lost cause. I stood from my desk, where I'd been trying to look busy, and rushed out of my office, meeting him at his door.

He wouldn't meet my eyes at first, his expression stern. When he opened his door, he pushed it forward. "Have a seat."

I did as I was told, sitting down in one of the black leather chairs in front of his desk. He took off his jacket, hanging it on the back of his chair and dusting off his sleeves before sitting down. It was once he was seated that he met my eye for the first time.

"I think we both know why we're here."

"Sir, if you'll just let me explain—"

"Explain what, Gates? Explain why you invited your friend to a very important dinner party for one of our biggest clients? Completely ignoring the fact that friends and family aren't allowed at the functions in the first place. Would you like to explain how you let him get so drunk that he told our best client, to her face, that you'd called her a bitch? Or maybe you'd like to explain why you felt like you should express that opinion about our best client to your friend in the first place." I flinched with every word he said, my shoulders slouching more and more.

"He wasn't supposed to be there. And I *hadn't* said that. Elias had had too much to drink. I was dealing with trying to make sure everything ran smoothly. I thought he'd already left, but…" I stopped, taking a deep breath. "Bringing him was a mistake. He wasn't invited, and he overstepped."

"Was he also not invited to the office a few nights before when you stole company property?"

"I…what?"

"The absolute lack of regard for company policies and rules—" Spittle formed in the corner of his mouth as his voice raised. "And to be so careless when we'd just had an attempted security breach, to bring people here, to steal property—"

"The CDs?" I asked, finally understanding what he was talking about. "I didn't mean to—"

"What didn't you mean to do, exactly? Because from the way it looked on the security tapes, you certainly didn't seem to have any reservations."

"They were old CDs from promos that wouldn't have been used anyway—"

He slammed his fist on top of the desk. "They *weren't* yours to take, is the entire point. Whether or not you thought they'd get used. They were given to the company, not to you." He took a deep breath, running his hands through his wild, gray hair. "Now, I was willing to over-look it, to let you explain yourself because you've been nothing if not loyal to this company, but after last night's events, I simply cannot overlook your actions any longer. I'll save you the embarrassment of having you clean out your things on Monday by staying for an hour until you can remove everything from your office today."

"Please, sir, you don't understand—"

"I understand plenty," he said. "And what I understand is that you've deliberately broken the rules *twice* now. Three times if we count the fact that you told your friend about our security issues in the first place. I was willing to let that slide because he offered his services for free, but I cannot and will not overlook anything else. Now, Layla has agreed to stay with the agency, but in order to make that happen, we have to let you go."

"Isn't there anything I can do to change your mind? I've done everything right by this company. You know how much it means to me. I'm so sorry. It was a mistake."

"Until these past few days, I thought I did know how much this all meant to you, yes. But now, you've proven me wrong. I'm sorry, Wes. My mind is made up. I need you to clean out your office quickly. I haven't been home in over twenty-four hours, and I'm exhausted." His expression softened. "If you go quietly, I'll give you a good reference wherever you apply next."

"I'll be starting over," I argued softly, no power to my words.

"It's the best I can do." He stood at that point, a hand held out as a gesture to let me know it was time to go. "If I were you, I'd take the offer and leave, before I change my mind."

I swallowed, my throat dry, chest tight. There was nothing left to do. Nothing to say that would change his mind. I stood, looking down at the carpeted floor for what would be the last time as I made my way across the small office and toward my own.

I'd lost everything in the blink of an eye.

How had things gone so wrong so quickly?

# CHAPTER TWENTY-FIVE

My entire life at the Noel DeMarcum Agency could be condensed into two cardboard boxes. Pictures, autographs—the ones made out to me, at least. I wasn't going to be accused of stealing again—and other personal effects. A mug, a jacket, an extra tie, two bags of tea, and a change of shoes.

I walked out of the office, leaving my keys and badge on the lateral filing cabinet next to my door without a word to my former boss. There was nothing left to say. Nothing that could be done.

As I loaded the boxes into the back seat of my car, I was hit with the sorrow-filled realization that all I wanted to do was call Addy and tell her what had happened. I wanted her to comfort me, to love me through it, but it wouldn't happen.

The truth was, I'd chosen my work over my wife, and in the end, they'd both left me.

I sat in the car, knowing that when I pulled out of the parking garage, it would be for the last time. Whatever my next step would be, I'd never come back to the company that had built me.

I put my head in my hands, trembling with overwhelming sorrow. No tears came, just pangs of fury mixed with terrible fear about what would happen to me. My bank account balance was dwindling, my wife hated me, and I had no job, no place to go…

As if to add insult to injury, a shrill beep sounded through the car, and when I looked up, I noted the low fuel light that had lit up on the dash.

The idea of staying with Elias, even for one more day, was impossible to stomach. What, then, were my options? I could go back to the motel, but my money would run out even sooner that way. I needed to find something to pay the bills that would stack up quickly. Though I hadn't made great money, my income had paid three-fourths of the bills. Addy was going to be devastated.

Disappointed in me.

What was new?

We'd never had a nest egg, always having to use whatever we'd saved to cover the latest emergency or expense. It wasn't easy to unbury yourself from debt when life was always at the top of the grave, shoveling new dirt on top of you.

The air conditioner had gone out one summer.

We'd needed new tires the next.

Rory had fractured her arm just before Christmas one year, and we'd had the car break down and need a new transmission just as soon as the debt had been paid off.

It seemed to be Murphy's Law, and now it was catching up with us, with me, tenfold.

The last place I wanted to go was back to Elias' apartment, but I needed to get my things. Even if I had to sleep in the guest bedroom, I was going to go back home. Addy could hate me all she wanted, but she wouldn't want me to be homeless. Besides, like it or not, we were in this together.

A few minutes later, after refilling the car's gas tank, I parked in the parking garage of Elias' apartment, almost feeling lighter about the idea of leaving the place for good. No matter what happened next, I would never have to see Elias again.

I climbed the stairs and slid my key in the lock, but the moment I opened it, my smile evaporated.

"*Addy?* What are you doing here?" Addy stood in front of me, Elias just to her left. "What is going on?"

She looked at him; he looked at me. "I invited Addy here so that we could talk to you."

"Talk about what?" I demanded, moving toward her to protect her from him. I reached for her, but she stepped back, shaking her head.

"Why don't you sit down?" she asked, but I didn't move.

*Not a chance in hell*, I wanted to say. I knew in my gut that something wasn't right, but I couldn't bear to take my eyes off of her long enough to form thoughts about what could be happening.

"Fine, you don't have to sit," Addy said, her voice honey sweet, as I'd often heard her when talking to Rory, but rarely me. "Elias contacted me this morning and said it was important that I come over so we could all sit down and talk things through."'

I nodded. "About Stephanie?"

Addy flinched at her name. "No," she said quickly. "No, this isn't about her, Wes. It's about you."

"What about me?"

Elias took a step toward me, his voice soft. "We're worried about you, Wes. I know you've been dealing with so much stress at work, and with the divorce—"

"You don't know what you're talking about." I hated the way they were both looking at me. "Stop looking at me like that!"

"I'm worried you're close to a breakdown," Elias said plainly. "I didn't know what else to do."

"Elias told me that you've been paranoid about people stealing your stuff... About him trying to impersonate you or-or take your job? He said that you've been angry and lashing out, and that you were fired last night? Tell me that's not true, Wes," Addy said, though she looked like she already believed it.

"How could you have known I was fired?" I asked him.

"You told me," he said, shaking his head. "Don't you remember?"

"I wasn't fired until this morning. You had no right to call her—"

"That's not what you said last night," he said, then looked at Addy. "See what I mean."

"Don't you start that!" I screamed, pointing my finger at him. "This is what he does. He," I put my hands on either temple, "he gets inside your head and tricks you. Just like he ate meat in front of me and then told me he was vegetarian. He's trying to make me think I'm going crazy!"

"Wes, listen," Addy said, stepping toward me, her eyes full of worry. "I know you're dealing with a lot, but you need to talk to us, okay? We only want to help. Why didn't you tell me things had gotten so bad?"

"I'm fine!" I screamed, pleading with them to believe me.

"Lashing out," Elias said, walking a circle around me. "It's a classic sign."

"What are you talking about? A classic sign of what?" I demanded.

"It doesn't matter," Addy said. "We just need to take this one step at a time, okay? Will you sit down for me?"

"Sit down? Addy, please, tell me what this is about. What does he have in your head? I'm fine, okay? I'm fine!"

"Have you been sleeping, Wes? Have you been eating normally?" Addy asked.

I nodded. "Yes."

At the same time, I saw Elias shake his head out of the corner of my eye.

"What the hell are you doing, man?" I asked, spinning around to look at him. "Why are you lying? Do you just get off on making me look crazy?" I looked back at Addy. "Did he tell you that the reason I accused him of trying to take over my life was because he stole my clothes? That he's wearing my cologne. He crashed my party at work last night, and that's why I got fired!" Addy glanced toward Elias, who pursed his lips as if to say *see what I mean.*

"No!" I screamed, shaking my head angrily. "This is not a thing. I'm not going crazy, Addy. I swear to you, I'm not. He's just trying to make it seem that way. You can't listen to him. He'll tear us apart if you let him." I heard how crazy I sounded, but I couldn't calm down. My heart raced in my chest, my palms sweating profusely. Why didn't she believe me?

"Okay, okay... Calm down. Let's calm down, okay? Elias is only trying to help. We just want to help."

"Help with what?"

"We think it's time you started talking to someone, Wes. A professional."

"A shrink?" I asked, swiping the back of my hand across my forehead.

"A therapist," Addy corrected. "Someone who can help you work through what you're going through."

"I'm going through a divorce, same as you. *You're* not seeing a therapist. Don't let him get in your head about this, Addy. It's me we're talking about. I'm fine."

"Wes, I only want to see you healthy. You know how much I love you. I don't want you to be sick. There's nothing wrong with seeking help. It makes you brave. Everyone gets a little off course sometimes."

"I'm not sick," I argued. "I'm fine. I just want to come home." My voice broke as I said the words, mostly from anger, but also from the truth in what I'd said. God, I just wanted to go home. I just wanted to get away from Elias, who was making me question if I was going crazy after all.

Addy nodded, reaching her hands up to take me in her arms. I rested my head on her shoulder, refusing to cry. "I'm so sorry. I'm so sorry about everything," I whispered, wanting the conversation to be just between us.

"I know you are," she said, her cheek rubbing against mine. "I know."

"She meant nothing to me, okay? Nothing. And I'm going to figure out a new job. I'll start applying right away. You've just gotta get me out of here. You've gotta let me come home. He's trying to make me crazy, Addy. Please don't listen to him. Please let's just go home."

"Okay." She patted the back of my head, squeezing me even tighter as she whispered softly in my ear. "It's okay. We don't have to talk about any of that right now. Just breathe. Elias, would you mind bringing him some water?"

"I don't want water. I just want to go. Please, let's go. Let's get my things, and let's just go." I looked over my shoulder toward Elias, who was calmly filling a glass with tap water. "Why are you doing this to me?"

"I'm not doing anything to you, Wes. I'm making a glass of water. If you don't want it—"

"You know exactly what you're doing," I lashed out. "*You're a psychopath*. You've been planning this all along, haven't you? You're enjoying this... You've always enjoyed it. All the best friend bullshit. You've just been playing me."

His eyes traveled to Addy, who turned my face back to hers. She held my cheeks between her hands, her warm eyes dancing between mine. "Your heart is racing, sweetheart. Just breathe with me, okay? We'll get your stuff, and we'll leave. You can come home with me. Just breathe though, okay? It's all going to be alright."

She inhaled deeply, and I followed her lead, my rage blurring my vision.

We exhaled together, our breath combining in the space between us. I focused on her eyes, on her words, soothing me.

It was all going to be okay.

I was going home.

We were going to be fine.

I hardly noticed Elias' footsteps behind me as he approached us, interrupting the quiet moment. Addy let go of my face, reaching for the glass of water and handing it to me. "Just take a drink of water, okay? Take a drink and let's all calm down, and then we can figure everything else out."

I eyed the drink suspiciously, which led her to sigh. "Would I let you take anything that wasn't safe?" She took a sip herself. "It's water, Wes. It's just water."

I took the glass from her hands, lifting the lukewarm beverage to my lips. I took a sip, then another, then downed the rest of the glass, unaware of how parched I was.

Once I'd emptied it, she handed it back to Elias, who returned it to the kitchen. "There now," she said, keeping her voice low. "Doesn't that already feel better? Why don't we go into your bedroom where we can talk, okay? Just the two of us."

I nodded. "Yeah, okay." She let go of my shoulders, taking my hand and leading me across the room. I pushed open the door and took a step into the bedroom, knowing it would be for the last time.

I was going home.

Then, I passed out.

# CHAPTER TWENTY-SIX

When I awoke, I heard the familiar *tick, tick, tick* of the fan above me, felt the warm, swirling air from its blades hitting my face.

Had it all been a dream? The room was pitch black, but I could see a hint of light coming from behind the curtains.

"I'm just so glad you've been here for him," I heard Addy say. "For us. Seriously, Elias, I'm not sure what I would've done without you."

I tried to sit up, to call out to her, but my throat was dry and my head was heavy. I felt the muscles in my neck tighten, a sign that my body was attempting to appease my wishes, but I couldn't move.

I took a deep breath, trying to roll myself off the bed. Before I could move even a single finger, darkness found me again.

# CHAPTER TWENTY-SEVEN

I wasn't sure how much time had passed before I found consciousness again, but when I came to, it was Elias' voice I heard, though I couldn't make out what he was saying. It was distant, further away than Addy's had been before. I smelled food... Pizza, perhaps.

He was laughing about something, and I heard her laughter, too.

What was funny?

Why weren't they helping me?

What was wrong with me?

Why couldn't I feel my body?

Then, darkness.

## CHAPTER TWENTY-EIGHT

The next time I awoke, Addy was standing at the side of the bed. I tried to find my focus as the blurry halo of her face hovered above me.

As my eyes blinked open, she leaned further down, her face coming into view, though there was still a strange blurriness to the edges of her skin. "Wes? Can you hear me? How are you feeling?" she asked. I felt her cool touch, a finger laid against my cheek. She trailed it down to my jawbone carefully.

I stared at her, the words forming in the back of my mind, though I couldn't force them forward. I wanted to answer her, to tell her we needed to leave, that something was wrong, that she should get help, but there was nothing there.

No part of my brain could turn thoughts to words.

It was as if that part had never existed at all.

Maybe it hadn't.

What was *exist* after all?

What was anything?

## CHAPTER TWENTY-NINE

"Oh, I don't know. I shouldn't leave him."

I heard the voice.

Addy's voice.

I moved to sit up with a painful jolt, surprised to see that my arms worked again. As if I'd been reconnected to my body somehow. Every movement was slow, my thoughts swimming through Jell-O, but they were there. I knew where I was.

The sun had begun to rise, peeking out between my curtains and blinding me every so often as they danced in the breeze from the fan.

"Come on, Ad," he called her, the use of the nickname on his lips making my stomach turn circles, "you've got to eat something besides pizza. We've been up all night. Let me take you out for breakfast. Coffee, at least. We'll just go right down the street. He won't even know we left."

"It just doesn't feel right..."

"Come on," he said with a giggle, and then I heard her giggling, too. "For old time's sake."

"Okay!" she cried. "Okay, you win." He'd been tickling her. It made me sick to think of his hands on her body. "For old time's sake."

I pictured him slinging his arm across her shoulders, my skin crawling at the image. My arms went stiff, and I collapsed under my weight, no longer able to prop myself up.

# CHAPTER THIRTY

They were quiet for a moment, and then I heard her say, "I just hate it."

I'd fallen asleep. I realized it then. I'd fallen asleep long enough for them to have had breakfast. They were back, the room was warmer, and I assumed it was around noon, the sun's rays beaming through the curtains at full force. The room was too warm, sweat beading at my hairline and in the small of my back, but I couldn't move. Addy was crying. Why was she crying?

"I can't believe I didn't see it."

"You can't blame yourself," Elias was saying. "You were doing the best you could." He paused.

"I'm so self-centered. I wasn't paying attention—"

"Hey, don't talk about yourself like that, okay? I think you're amazing, Addy. I always have."

"Thank you," she whispered, so low I almost didn't hear it. "But I failed him. I *broke* him. What if I did this somehow? What if it's all my fault?"

"No, no, no you didn't. This isn't your fault. You

couldn't control it or prevent it… You can't think like that. Trust me, it'll destroy you."

"Maybe there's something wrong with me…" More sobs.

"There's nothing wrong with you," he said, his voice dripping with admiration. It made my skin crawl. I felt my stomach tighten with sudden nausea.

"How do you explain it, then? The two men I've loved in my life, and they've both… How could I not see the signs in either of them?"

"Noah wasn't your fault," he said, and the name struck something in me. What was it? I closed my eyes, trying to think. It was as if I were trying to shock my brain back to life.

"I loved him. You know I did," she said. "I would've done anything to have helped him."

"It wasn't your fault," he repeated more firmly. "The depression was too much for him. We tried, we all tried… It wasn't anyone's fault. But, look at it this way, it could've saved Wes. What we went through because of Noah, it might be the only thing that saves Wes. Because I recognized the signs—the paranoia, the highs and lows—we can get him the help he needs. There's a really great center a few hours from here. I can call them if you'd like."

"Do you really think he needs that? I mean, a therapist and some medication. From the research I've done, I think, given enough time and the right combination, he could be okay."

"I hope you're right, I'd just hate to know we didn't do all we could for him."

I shuddered, listening to them talk. I wasn't depressed.

I wasn't paranoid. I wanted to scream it at them. Why couldn't Addy see what he was doing? Why hadn't I seen it coming?

The memory of Noah came back to me all at once, the fog clearing. He'd been Addy's boyfriend before me.

A boy who'd taken his own life in junior high.

As the memories flooded me, I remembered the memorial service we'd had for him in the school gymnasium. The counselors they'd called in to talk to us all and help us work through the grief and confusion.

*Noah Munn.*

His full name hit me swiftly.

Elias' brother.

No wonder he'd been so quiet in school. Of course, I remembered now. Really remembered. He wasn't just the shy kid. The smart kid.

He was the kid living in his brother's shadow.

The kid living in the wake of his brother's death.

"You're right, of course," she said. "We have to do everything we can. I'd never forgive myself if..." She trailed off. "I need him to get better, so whatever you think will help. The clinic sounds nice. Thank you again for talking me through this. I seriously don't know what I'd do without you, Elias."

"Of course. I'm always going to be here for you, Addy. Always. I'm just so glad we found each other again."

She didn't respond, and I felt my stomach tighten with a wave of nausea again. This time, my body went cold and I knew I was going to be sick, but I couldn't move. I turned my head slightly, so the vomit wouldn't suffocate me.

Instead, the foamy bile spewed down my cheek and onto the comforter next to me. I coughed, trying to catch my breath as I felt a new wave coming over me. Again, my body tightened, and I felt the vomit rise in my throat. Just as it left my mouth, the door opened, Addy and Elias hurried toward my bedside, summoned by the noise.

Addy's face fell, and she looked across the room. "Do you have a washcloth?" she asked Elias, who sprang into action and made it across the room. I heard him sifting around in the bathroom, and a few moments later, he reappeared, handing her the cloth.

She wiped up my face gently, the smell permeating the room. Though I knew she could smell it, she didn't make a face or mention it at all. "Here you go. It's okay. Let's get you cleaned up. Do you think you can stand?"

I tried, but my body was no longer my own. It wouldn't move, wouldn't respond to my mental commands. I stared at her, blinking slowly. "Okay, that's okay," she said finally. "You don't have to. I'll just get you cleaned up this way." She dutifully wiped up the vomit, walking back and forth to the bathroom and returning with a rinsed cloth each time.

When she disappeared the last time, having cleaned up the remainder of the vomit, I heard her in the bathroom, rinsing out the cloth. "Do you think he got too hot? Maybe we should turn the heat down a bit," she called.

"Yeah, that's a good idea," Elias said, and I realized he was standing right behind me. My body went numb with fear as I tried to turn my head to look at him.

I strained, trying desperately to sit up as sheer terror swam through me.

What was he going to do? Surely nothing with her standing just feet away.

I needed to move. I didn't want her to see me like this. I didn't want to be the bed-ridden husband while Elias swooped in and pretended to save the day. But I couldn't move.

I felt something sharp prick my hip without warning, my body going rigid from the pain. It was white-hot and electrifying, but over in seconds. A shot of some sort.

I felt Elias' hands on my hip. He patted my side, lifting the edge of my pants back up.

What had he done?

What had he given me?

My vision began to grow fuzzy almost immediately. I needed to tell Addy what had happened.

When her footsteps approached me again, I could no longer see her. The room around me was dark.

No, my eyes were closed without me realizing it.

I was fading fast…

"He's so tired," she said sadly in a huff. "Are you sure we don't need to call a doctor? He's practically slept for the last twenty-four hours."

"He's crashing after not having slept for a week, probably. Trust me, this is normal. We used to call them *dark days* with Noah, the low lows after the highest of highs. Let him sleep for a while. Then we can take him to the doctor once he's back to feeling like himself. Trust me, we're not going to be able to get him out of bed right now. He needs to recover."

"It's just not like him. I can't believe it's gotten so bad…"

"It comes on suddenly sometimes, and when you don't recognize the symptoms, or when you're not looking for them, it can seem sort of normal. You probably just thought he was working so much because he loved it, when it was really a symptom of his mania," Elias was saying as I felt the fuzzy darkness engulf my brain, wrapping its spindly fingers around my consciousness. "Don't worry. I'm here now. You're not in this alone anymore, Addy. You have me. I'm not going anywhere. We're going to take good care of him."

# CHAPTER THIRTY-ONE

When I came to, it was dark again. I'd given up trying to decipher how many hours or days had passed since my last awake time. Elias was coming in every few hours, under the guise of checking on me, or giving me a drink, and pricking me with whatever he kept sticking in my hip.

Whatever it was, it was powerful enough to keep me immobile entirely, though there were a few times when I'd wake up and feel my fingers tingling. I knew then that he'd waited longer in between doses. If he waited just a bit longer, I'd be able to wake myself up. I'd be able to move.

I'd be able to save myself.

But, like clockwork, he was back. Sometimes I was awake. Sometimes I was half asleep.

This time, though, with my fingers tingling and my eyes open, Elias was nowhere to be found.

I turned my head slowly, my muscles sore from going unused for so long. The apartment was silent all around me. I listened for their voices, for a sign that they were okay. That I wasn't alone. That she was still with me. But it never came.

I wiggled my toes, tilting my head to look down at them.

If Elias hadn't given me another dose, I had to believe something was wrong. Where were they?

Maybe he'd forgotten. Maybe they were asleep and he'd missed the newest dose. Maybe she was gone, and he didn't need to keep up the ruse any longer. If I had a chance, this was it.

I eased one hand up, placing my palm on the stiff comforter, then the next. Once they were both at my sides, I pushed up. The room spun around me.

My throat was sore, and I felt like I hadn't had anything to drink in weeks. I eased myself forward, sliding my feet onto the ground. They were heavy, landing with a thud. I sat still, waiting to see if I'd given myself up. I'd expected the noise to alert them that I was awake, expected to hear them rushing toward me at any moment, but instead, I was met with more silence.

That worried me more. I stiffened my back, my spine cracking loudly as I did. I looked over my shoulder, searching for my phone. If I could find it, I could call the police.

When I stood, it took me several minutes to regain equilibrium, the entire world tilting on its axis around me. I was exhausted and weak. My stomach was sore and empty, and I felt nauseous again.

I bit down, refusing to give in to the urge to vomit. I had to keep it together. I grabbed hold of the footboard and took slow, quiet steps across the room. My phone wasn't lying on the nightstand. I leaned down, looking under the bed, my head jolting with the sudden move.

The phone wasn't there, so I stood up, gripping the footboard with both hands. I couldn't breathe. I couldn't catch my breath.

I needed to keep moving. I had one chance to get myself out, and I couldn't blow it.

I gripped the door knob, placing my other hand on the doorframe. My heart pounded, both from my nerves and from the jarring reality of being awake after having slept for so long.

With one swift motion, I swung the door open, staring around the dark living room. I shuffled my feet across the floor, trying to make sense of everything. Moonlight lit the room, casting shadows across the furniture.

Addy wasn't there.

Neither was Elias.

Where were they?

I felt my gaze being drawn across the room to Elias' door. Could they be in there...together? She wouldn't, would she?

No.

Please no.

She didn't see the wolf in sheep's clothing. If they were so close before, if she trusted him now, perhaps she'd let her guard down. Perhaps she needed someone to comfort her through the hardship that was taking care of me. Elias, I was sure, was more than happy to oblige.

I shuffled my feet quicker, my hand resting on the wall as I made my way across the apartment and toward the door. I no longer cared about them hearing me. I had to get to her. I had to save her.

When I reached the door, I turned the knob, pushing it open and flipping on the light.

I sucked in a deep breath.

The bed was empty.

Elias was gone.

Addy was gone.

# CHAPTER THIRTY-TWO

The room smelled stale. The smell of cologne had faded, replaced by sweat and cleaner, though it was every bit as dirty as it had been the last time I'd been in there. I looked all around, searching for a sign as to where they were.

"Addy?" I called out, though I knew it was useless. They were gone. They'd left me. I had no idea what he'd done with my wife, where he'd taken her. I screamed with rage and kicked the mattress, the motion with my unstable footing knocking me down. From where I sat on the floor, I pulled his sheets off the bed, tossing things across the room, angry tears blurring my vision. I was a toddler having a tantrum, wanting to destroy the things that belonged to my enemy.

Where were they?

Where had he taken her?

I'd never been so angry.

Never quaked with white-hot fury like I was in that moment.

I needed to find her.

I needed to find a phone.

I eased myself onto my hands and knees, reaching for the mattress to help me stand up. When I did, I froze, spying a box underneath the computer desk on his far wall. It was simple cardboard, no identifying features, but something about it made the hairs on my arms stand up.

I scooted myself forward, *one hand, one knee, one hand, one knee,* until I reached the desk. I shoved the chair out of the way, my movements still clumsy as I pulled it toward me. Sitting back on my butt, I tossed the lid off the box, digging inside. The box contained several yearbooks, newspaper clippings, and loose photos.

It took a moment for me to process what I was seeing, but once I had, I felt myself sobering up almost instantly, the outright fear was ice cold in my veins.

The photos, snapshots of Addy and me—or, my body at least. On each one—photos of prom and our wedding, and then more recently of us at the park, us out with Rory —he'd replaced my head with his own, taping a picture of his grinning face where mine had once been.

I dropped the pictures, one by one, with shaking hands, my stomach churning.

No.

No.

No.

No.

There was a wedding announcement, though he'd scribbled out my name and face, replacing both with his own. Rory's birth announcement, his own name replacing mine there, too.

There was a plain, spiral-bound notebook near the bottom that I dragged out, then dropped as if it were on fire, the book landing open in front of me. Each of the one hundred and twenty pages were lined with scrawled-out handwriting.

*Mrs. Addison Munn.*

*Mrs. Addison Munn.*

*Mrs. Addison Munn.*

I threw the book across the room, trembling as I returned to the photos, each one more terrifying than the last as I realized what a monster I was truly dealing with. Even I hadn't suspected it was this bad.

When I'd gone through all the loose photos, I opened the yearbook, almost too afraid to look. I flipped until I found Addy's photo. The page was sticky and stiff, and he'd drawn several hearts around her face. I fought back bile as it rose in my throat, my vision blurring with fury-filled tears.

I flipped back a page, using a single finger to turn it, and checked for my picture. He'd scribbled out my face to the point that the paper had torn.

I looked down, to where someone just below me had been scribbled through, too, so much so that I had to look at their name to see who it was.

*Noah Munn.*

His own brother?

I felt sick.

I tossed the yearbook in the direction of the notebook, pulling out another.

And another.

And another.

Each year, Addy had hearts, and I was scribbled out. Each year until his brother had passed away, he too was scribbled out. I trembled with trepidation as I closed the last book, both wanting and not wanting to know what other secrets the box might hold.

I flipped through pages and pages of photographs— candid shots he'd managed to snap of us. At restaurants, through the open windows of our house, at a neighbor's barbecue and an art gallery event I'd dragged Addy to at the last minute. So many moments… In each one, his face replaced mine. With each one, the sick feeling in my stomach grew stronger and stronger. How long had he been watching us? Following us?

When I reached the bottom of the box, I sat in horror, looking around at all the evidence that had been just under my nose. It was then that I realized it had never been about me. He wasn't ruining my life because of anything I'd done. It was always Addy.

He was obsessed with her.

He was deranged.

Everything he'd done…it was always just about him trying to get me out of the way. Inviting me to move in, ruining my life, making Addy believe I was crazy. He'd seen his chance and swooped in immediately.

Another sick thought hit me. Had he done the same thing to his brother? Had he been willing to do whatever it took to get Addy back then, too?

I stood up on shaky legs, clicking his mouse to open the computer, hoping it might give me some clue as to where they'd gone. Maybe he'd searched an address or… bought a plane ticket. The idea was terrifying. When the computer lit up, the screen caused me to jump back. His wallpaper was a collage of photos of her, some candid, some posed. I spied a few of our wedding photos where he'd edited me out.

I tapped the mouse, cursing when I realized the computer was locked. I tried to think.

*Addy,* I typed. The box buzzed, letting me know it was wrong.

*Addison*, I tried again. Still wrong.

I tried her birthday.

Her full name.

Then, I thought of the notebook. *Mrs. Addison Munn.*

Success. The darkened screen disappeared, allowing me access to his computer, but what I saw was completely and utterly terrifying. I backed away as though I'd been shoved, a scalding-hot wave of disbelief washing over me.

The screen was like a beehive, small square sections all around. There were at least twenty of them.

Each box was a separate camera. And each camera was spying on us.

There was one that appeared to be in the corner of the bedroom he'd given me, a hidden camera placed just above my bed, with a bird's-eye view of the entire room, but that was far from the most sinister. One gave a clear view into my old bedroom, Addy's and mine, and I knew the view was from the computer across from our bed. I spied the photo of us propped up on her nightstand, next to where her head rested each night, and realized she'd taken it from its place on the wall and moved it there, closer to her. A lump rose in my throat. *She'd missed me.* Though I wanted to savor the moment, the outright horror I felt wouldn't allow me to. The camera he'd labeled **A's phone** gave a darkened view of what appeared to be the inside of her purse. My stomach rolled, and I put a hand to my mouth as my eyes processed the next one: Rory's bedroom. Rory's bed. The view of Rory's ceiling came from the camera labeled **R's phone**. My hands clenched into shaking fists as fuzzy patches clouded my vision. I gritted my teeth so hard I winced, looking at the next one. The box labeled **W's phone** gave a darkened view of what appeared to be the inside of Addison's vehicle. There was a camera with a view of Addy's classroom. One in my old office. I forced myself to look away, unable to catch my breath. It wasn't possible and yet, it was all real. Straight from a nightmare.

I remembered Elias' warnings then, about webcams and being careful, and it all began to click into place. I remembered tearing the blue sticky note off the day after he'd placed it there, thinking he was ridiculous.

He wasn't trying to protect me. He was teasing me, playing games that I hadn't realized he was playing.

He'd hacked our webcams. Our phone cameras. He'd been watching us at home, at work... Everywhere. He knew our every move.

He hadn't just happened to run into me that day. It had been his plan for years.

All our lives.

He'd just been waiting for the perfect time to make a move.

# CHAPTER THIRTY-THREE

The one good thing about having access to the webcams, once I'd gotten over the initial horror, was that I could tell where they were. When I clicked on the camera that belonged to Addy's phone, I could hear her voice as she led him into the house.

Our house.

"I just don't want to be gone for too long," she was saying. It was terrifying how clearly he could hear us. How long had he been listening? What all had he heard? "In case he wakes up." Why didn't they warn people this kind of thing could happen?

"I agree," he was saying. "Dr. Foster just wants us to get a few things of his from home that will make him feel more comfortable once he gets to the hospital tomorrow. Maybe like a photograph or something sentimental."

*No.*

"I'm sure I have something around here," she said. "Just be quiet. My mother and Rory are both asleep. I haven't told them what's going on. I don't know how to… I'm not sure what to say."

They walked in front of the camera in our bedroom, and I clicked on that one, listening in. I could no longer see them as they were out of view, but I listened closely.

"I understand," he was saying. They were quiet for a bit, and then I heard him say, "She could be your twin, you know? She looks just like the way I remember you from back then."

She laughed softly. "Thank you. I get that a lot, but I see her dad in her more. She has his smile."

"No, no… It's all you."

"That's what they tell me."

He didn't respond right away.

"She's beautiful, you know?" he said, his voice a low growl.

"Thank you," she said, something in her tone stiffening. "So, what do you think about this picture to send with him?"

He didn't answer.

After a moment, she said, "Elias? Where did you go —*ah!*"

She screamed, and I heard a thud. "Addy!" I cried, though it was no use. No one could hear me. I was invisible. A fly on the wall.

I watched him move past the webcam, a blur of black.

He was leaving. What had he done? I put a hand over my lips as I tried to think of what to do. I clicked away from the camera, back to the hive-like screen, and saw him come into view in another one moments later. *Rory's bedroom.*

His words echoed in my head as realization flooded me.

*She could be your twin, you know?*

He wasn't after Addy anymore.

He wanted her as she was before.

He wanted Rory.

I watched my daughter sit up in bed. She rubbed her eyes gently, pulling the cover up over herself, seeming to sense the danger she was in. I stood from the chair as I heard her voice, wanting to run to her and not wanting to move at the same time.

"Mom?" she asked, her voice hoarse from sleep. When she processed the sight of him, she cocked her head to the side. "Brody? What are you... What are you doing here?"

*Brody?* I felt myself grow dizzy as I recognized the name.

# CHAPTER THIRTY-FOUR

I didn't know what to do. No choice made sense as I made my way out of the apartment, not even bothering to close the door behind me. I didn't have a phone, didn't have a wallet, but I had my keys. I had to act quickly.

I was wobbly on my feet, my head still fuzzy, but I had no time to slow down. I climbed in the car, zipping out of the parking garage and onto the street. I hurried out of downtown, pressing the accelerator to the floor as I hit the interstate.

I needed to call the police, but I couldn't stop. I didn't have a phone. I had to get there. I just had to keep moving.

Faster.

Faster.

I turned on the icy air conditioning, trying to keep myself awake as I felt a wave of exhaustion sweep over me. I had to get to Rory. I had to get to Addy.

I wasn't crazy.

I'd never been crazy.

Elias was everything I'd thought he was and so much more.

Now, my family needed me, and it was up to me to save them.

When I arrived at the house fifteen minutes later, it was a complete miracle that I was still standing. I leapt from the car, barreling up the stairs with my key at the ready. I stuck it in the lock, opening the door swiftly.

*"What do you want from me?"* I heard as I opened the door. Rory was crying, her voice too loud for him to hear all the noise that I was making. I rushed through the living room, into the hall. "Please don't do this. You don't have to do this. I don't want to go with you. Please. My parents will be home any minute. My grandmother's right down the hall. They won't let me go with you."

Without a hint of reservation, I shoved into her bedroom, and Elias turned around, his eyes wild.

*"What the—"*

I leapt at him, no qualms about sensical actions as I rammed him into the wall. Rory was on her bed. She'd changed out of her pajamas into everyday clothing and had a suitcase open on her bed, one she was reluctantly packing with clothing. When she realized what was happening, she dropped the stack of T-shirts in her hand and cried, *"Daddy, I'm sorry."*

"Get your mom!" I screamed. "Call the police and lock the door behind you! Get out of here." She darted from the room, though she glanced behind her once hesitantly, as Elias jammed his elbow into my side.

*"Go!"* I screamed through the pain.

"I'm not sure how you managed to find me," Elias said,

standing up as I covered my side with my hands in pain. "You were supposed to be taking a nice, long nap." He lifted his foot, ramming it into my stomach, and I doubled over. He turned away from me, moving to walk out of the room, but I grabbed his feet, holding on for dear life. He stumbled, but didn't fall, trying to kick himself free. His fingers found my eyes, shoving into them, and I screamed, pulling my head back but refusing to let go.

"Stay the hell away from my family," I roared, jerking us backward so he fell on top of me. We both cried out, though he recovered quicker. The room had begun to go fuzzy for me, my eyes throbbing.

"You had everything, Wes," he snarled. "Everything, and you still managed to screw it all up. You don't deserve her. You don't deserve any of them. I couldn't let you keep hurting her. It was killing me." He moved to stand up, and I swung my arm, connecting with his teeth.

I watched the blood coat his teeth quickly, but he merely smiled, swiping the back of his hand across his mouth. He stood and I reached for his legs, but he stepped out of the way, too fast for me.

"Leave them alone!" I screamed.

He opened the door, and I heard a *crack*, then saw his body fall down, his hands grasping at his knee. "What the fuck?" he screamed, writhing on the floor as blood spilled out onto the carpet.

Vivienne stood there, a gun in her hand, and a terrified-but-triumphant look on her face. "Wes!" she cried, holding out a hand for me. I shoved myself up off the carpet, darting past Elias as he screamed, trying to stand up, but failing.

I reached my mother-in-law, wrapping an arm around her waist and leading her down the hallway as quickly as we could move. "Rory, let us in," I cried when we reached the locked bedroom. "Come on, it's Dad."

I heard the soft click, and she pulled the door open just as I heard Elias began to slide his way out of the room. I looked back, seeing his bloody hand creeping out into the hallway. Pushing Vivienne into the room first, then shutting the door behind us, I grabbed Rory and kissed her head.

Addison was on the floor still, though I saw no blood. I had to believe, to hope, that he'd given her something similar to what he'd given me. I heard Elias scream out, the sound getting closer, and pushed us all to hide on the opposite side of the bed, dragging Addy's body to join us.

"I called the police," Vivienne said, her voice shaky and breathless. "It shouldn't be long now."

"Thank you," I said, hoping it could encompass everything I had to be thankful for at that moment. I ran a hand over Addy's chest.

"She's breathing," Rory told me, her voice a high-pitched whine. "She just won't wake up."

"It's okay," I said, hoping it was true. "It's all going to be okay." I found a strange sense of calm in the moment, even as Elias grew closer outside of the door. I could hear the sounds of him dragging himself down the hall, the noise getting louder as he grew near. Vivienne eyed me and then looked down at the gun, a confirmation in her eyes.

"I'm so sorry, Dad," Rory cried, burying her face in my chest.

"It's okay. It's not your fault. None of this is your fault," I said, wanting to say so much more. There was so much to tell her. So much I needed to say, but all I wanted to do was hold her. So, that's what I did. I held her tightly with one arm and held Addy's hand with the other as we bunkered down there, the gun in Vivienne's hand, and Elias' screams filling the house as we waited for the police to get there.

We were together. That was all that mattered.

And I knew then and there, as I held my family close, I'd never give anyone the chance to take them from me again.

# CHAPTER THIRTY-FIVE

**SIX MONTHS LATER**

I walked into the concrete room where I'd see Elias for the first time since that horrible night. Over the last few months, we'd learned the truth, some of it by piecing it together ourselves, some of it from the police.

Elias had been stalking us since we'd left high school. He'd been obsessed with Addy even then. I was still convinced that he may have had something to do with his brother's death, but the police had assured me they had more than enough to focus on without reopening a case from more than twenty years ago.

Starting with the web cameras illegally spying on us, and the fact that they'd been able to trace the company's hack back to Elias' computer and found the cloning software from my phone on his computer. Also that they'd found all the messages he'd sent my fourteen-year-old daughter, pretending to be a teenage boy himself, as well as an entire pharmacy's worth of drugs stashed in his closet...*enough to tranquilize several horses for several weeks*, in the words of the officer I'd spoken to.

The list went on and on.

We'd learned that the drugs had come from Garth, Elias' dealer and only true friend, who'd been in on the whole thing.

Mac, Ariel, and Stephanie weren't Elias' friends at all. They were people he knew through the gaming community, but they'd barely known Elias before he'd hired them to ruin my life. It was Mac who had posed as "Matt," Brody's dad, the plan elaborate and cleverly executed.

Rory had admitted to us later that he'd told her he was twenty-one, which was why we hadn't met him. They'd been talking for more than two years.

He'd been laying the groundwork, spying on us, and setting his plan in motion for even longer, all our lives, practically.

The police said we may never know the extent of what he'd done, the level to which the madness had descended.

Everything that had happened, he'd planned.

Everything.

At the end of the day, his main goal was to get to Rory, but I had to believe he wanted to punish me as well. He believed Addy belonged to him. That I'd stolen her from him. He wouldn't have been satisfied until he'd stolen everything from me—my family, my job, and even my sanity—and he'd nearly succeeded.

The police assured us we were safe. That they had enough evidence to make sure Elias was never going to go free again, but that did little to calm our nerves.

We'd gotten rid of our computers and switched to

basic phones, and after I left the prison that day, we were moving far away and changing our names. Vivienne would come with us, too. After how she'd saved my life, all of our lives, we owed her that much.

For all his effort, Elias had saved my marriage rather than ruined it. Surviving what we'd been through had strengthened the bond between Addy and me. We were back to our old selves, yet brand new at the same time, the reality of what we'd almost lost crystal clear to us now. We'd never allow ourselves to forget the reasons we fought for the life we'd built together, and the new life we'd build in our future home.

I couldn't help but be thankful for the fact that Elias' obsession was what had saved us. Not only my marriage, but, most importantly, my daughter's life. Without his cameras, there was no way I would've made it in time. Without all the evidence on his computer, it may have been harder to nab him for his crimes.

The police still don't know what he was planning to do with Rory once he'd finished with me, only that he'd told her to get dressed and pack a bag because they were leaving. He'd been so close to stealing her away from me...

Maybe he would've kept up the ruse forever. Lived the rest of his life as Brody. I couldn't bear to think of it. If she'd packed faster, or if he hadn't had her pack at all... There was a good chance Elias would be somewhere in the world with my baby girl, and I'd have no idea how to find her.

As I sat down at the counter, the door beyond the glass opened, and he walked in. He'd lost weight, his skin sallow and sagging off the bone. His eyes were dark as if he hadn't slept in days. Maybe he hadn't.

When he saw me, a sly smile lifted one corner of his mouth. He sank down in the chair across from me, lifting the phone to his ear. I did the same, his breath on the other end of the line sending chills across my skin.

"I didn't think you'd come," he whispered. How had I never seen the pure evil that lingered behind his eyes?

"This is the only time I'll be here."

"Oh, no. You don't want to come visit me?" he teased. "I thought you were my best friend."

I clenched my fist involuntarily. "You're never going to see us again. Do you hear me? Rory. Addy. We're moving. You're stuck in here, and we're out there. You'll never see us again. Your plan failed, Elias. You failed."

"Are you sure about that?" he asked, his voice a low growl. "You're acting a little bit crazy right now. Maybe you should lie down." He winked.

"Play your mind games all you want. It doesn't matter to me. *I won.* Do you hear me, Elias? I won, and you're stuck in here. You thought you could break me. You thought you could ruin me, but I won."

He chuckled, the sound growing into a full-blown laugh.

I smacked my hand on the glass. "What the hell are you laughing about?"

"You think you're free, but you're not. You never will be, Wes. Don't you get it? How will you ever feel safe? How often do you check over your shoulder, wondering if I'm watching you? How many cameras do you think you'll be able to avoid forever? All of them? Even the ones you don't know exist? I'll get out of here someday, and I'll find you... Maybe I'll look a little different then. Maybe I'll be calling you father-in-law by then."

"You'll never—" I smacked the glass, standing from my seat, but stopped, lowering my voice. I couldn't let him get to me. That wasn't why I was there.

I swallowed, watching the evil expression bring life to his face as I took a seat. "You'll never get out of here. You went too far, Elias. You're done. You'll never have her." I didn't know who I was talking about—both of them, maybe.

His cocky grin made me sick. "You think you're rid of me, but you don't know the half of it. She was mine the day I met her, and she'll always be mine," he said. "I'll never stop. Not until I take my last breath. So, feel free to run, Wes. Run away. But just know that I haven't ever given up, and I won't ever give up... I'll be watching you again soon."

It was my turn to laugh. "Actually, *I* will be watching *you*, Elias."

It caught him off guard, his brow bouncing up.

"Oh, that's right, I didn't tell you. I figured out what I'm going to do now that I'm not with the agency, and the best part is that I get to do it from wherever I am. Anywhere in the world."

"What are you talking about?" he sneered.

"See, it just so happens that I've been able to land a remote security monitoring position for this place. They needed someone to keep an eye on the prisoners...let them know when they've done something wrong so they can punish them. They have cameras everywhere here...

The showers, the halls… Everywhere you go, I'll be watching and reporting. There's no privacy here, Elias. No secret room where you can be alone and live out your fucked-up fantasy. Well, unless you mean solitary confinement." I stood up, tapping the counter. "I've heard that place can make a person go crazy… Gee, I hope you don't have to spend any time in there."

He swallowed, his Adam's apple bobbing as I lowered the phone slowly, letting what I'd said sink in. It was the first time I'd ever seen him look scared of anything. I spun around, walking away from him with a growing grin.

What I'd said wasn't true, but that wasn't what mattered.

He believed me. I'd seen it in his eyes.

I'd scared *him* for once.

He could live out his time with that niggle of fear in the back of his mind.

The guard opened the door, and I walked through, a free man.

*Who's paranoid now, bitch?*

DON'T MISS THE NEXT
PSYCHOLOGICAL THRILLER FROM
KIERSTEN MODGLIN

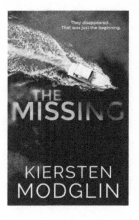

They disappeared...
That was just the beginning.

Order *The Missing* today:
mybook.to/MissingKModglin

## ENJOYED THE ROOMMATE?

If you enjoyed this story, please consider leaving me a quick review. It doesn't have to be long—just a few words will do. Who knows? Your review might be the thing that encourages a future reader to take a chance on my work!
To leave a review, please visit:
mybook.to/theroommate

Let everyone know how much you loved
*The Roommate* on Goodreads:
https://bit.ly/2Nj6PiG

## DON'T MISS THE NEXT RELEASE
## FROM KIERSTEN MODGLIN!

Thank you so much for reading this story. I'd love to invite you to sign up for my mailing list and text alerts so we can be sure you don't miss my next release.

Sign up for my mailing list here:
http://eepurl.com/dhiRRv
Sign up for my text alerts here:
www.kierstenmodglinauthor.com/textalerts.html

# ACKNOWLEDGMENTS

First and foremost, to my amazing husband and beautiful little girl—thank you for believing in me with everything you have. Thanks for celebrating each success and supporting me through every failure. I love you both so much.

To my friend, Emerald O'Brien—thank you for being my sounding board, for the laughs, and all of the advice.

To my immensely talented editor, Sarah West—thank you for always asking the hard questions and helping me to find the story I'm trying to tell through the mess.

To the proofreading team at My Brother's Editor— thank you for always finding those pesky typos and for keeping me laughing during the final stages.

To my loyal readers—thank you for being excited for each new story without hesitation. Thank you for the emails, the social media posts, the reviews, the recommendations, and the book club invitations. I'm so incredibly grateful to every single one of you.

To Vivienne "Vivi" Shininger, a reader who won the

chance to be featured in this story—thank you for your support. I hope you love your character!

To some of my biggest cheerleaders—Joy Westerfield, Sarah DeLong, Katy Corbeil, Shelly Reynolds, Renee Tucci, Phyllis Pisanelli, Lisa Hemming, Serena Soape, Carrie Shields, April Rose, Shannon Jump, Crystal Wilke, AJ Campbell, Amber Rexrode, Sherry Sias, Donna Beiderman, Susan Alford, Sara Booth, and so many others (I know I'm forgetting too many!), thank you for cheering the loudest, for all the tags, photos, and reviews, and for believing in my stories as much as I do.

Last but certainly not least, to you—thank you for reading this story. Whether this is your first Kiersten Modglin novel, or your twenty-third, I hope it was everything you hoped for and nothing like you expected. Thank you for supporting art and allowing me to get these crazy stories out of my head.

# ABOUT THE AUTHOR

Kiersten Modglin is an Amazon Top 30 bestselling author of psychological thrillers, a member of International Thriller Writers and the Alliance of Independent Authors, a KDP Select All-Star, and a ThrillerFix Best Psychological Thriller Award Recipient. Kiersten grew up in rural Western Kentucky with dreams of someday publishing a book or two. With more than twenty-five books published to date, Kiersten now lives in Nashville, Tennessee with her husband, daughter, and their two Boston Terriers: Cedric and Georgie. She is best known for her unpredictable psychological suspense. Kiersten's work is currently being translated into multiple languages and readers across the world refer to her as 'The Queen of Twists.' A Netflix addict, Shonda Rhimes super-fan, psychology fanatic, and indoor enthusiast, Kiersten enjoys rainy days spent with her nose in a book.

Sign up for Kiersten's newsletter here:
http://eepurl.com/b3cNFP

Sign up for text alerts from Kiersten here:
www.kierstenmodglinauthor.com/textalerts.html

www.kierstenmodglinauthor.com
www.facebook.com/kierstenmodglinauthor
www.facebook.com/groups/kmodsquad
www.twitter.com/kmodglinauthor
www.instagram.com/kierstenmodglinauthor
www.tiktok.com/@kierstenmodglinauthor
www.goodreads.com/kierstenmodglinauthor
www.bookbub.com/authors/kiersten-modglin
www.amazon.com/author/kierstenmodglin

# ALSO BY KIERSTEN MODGLIN

The Healer (The Messes, #2)

The Liar (The Messes, #3)

The Prisoner (The Messes, #4)

## NOVELLAS

The Long Route: A Lover's Landing Novella

The Stranger in the Woods: A Crimson Falls Novella

## THE LOCKE INDUSTRIES SERIES

The Nanny's Secret

Made in United States
North Haven, CT
22 April 2024

51636890R00171